Awards & Publication Acknowledgments
for
Naked, with Glasses

Awards

• Short story Collection *Naked, with Glasses,* Grand Prize, UKA [United Kingdom Authors] Press International Writing Competition, 2007

• "Naked, with Glasses," 3rd Prize, "Seven Deadly Sins Contest," *Story Magazine,* 1995

Publication Acknowledgments

Portions of *Naked, with Glasses* have appeared previously (sometimes in altered form or under different titles, and under the name "Sherri" Szeman) in the following publications:

Journals

• *Roanoke Review* (Roanoke College)

• *Soundings East* (Salem State College)

• *Tennessee Quarterly* (Belmont University)

• *Wisconsin Review*

• *Writers' Forum* (University of Colorado)

About
Naked, with Glasses
(award-winning stories)

Szeman began writing short stories at 12. A voracious reader who'd wanted to be an author since the age of 6, she knew all about books. She promptly began designing covers for her stories, stapling them into book format, and trying to sell them for the unbelievably incredible bargain-basement price of only 25¢. Though there were no buyers for these limited edition stories — now, unfortunately, all lost — Szeman was not discouraged. Only months later, she was writing love poetry, after having memorized Shakespeare's *Romeo & Juliet*, and passing them out to anyone who'd accept them. Sort of like a street-vendor hawking a show in New York.

❀

Eventually, her poetry became more sophisticated and she began getting acceptances and awards from literary journals. Though she published her first novel before she wrote her first successful short story, she'd mastered the craft. Her very first story (as an adult) was the title story of this collection, "Naked, with Glasses," which was awarded Third Prize in *Story Magazine*'s "Seven Deadly Sins Contest," and begins with the crowd-pleasing line: "This is how the plan to kill your husband could begin."

After her initial success, Szeman turned more often to short stories: whenever the subject matter was too long or inappropriate for poetry, or far too short for a novel-length treatment. Entertaining crowds at bookstore readings and writing conferences with her stories, she eventually had enough for a collection. Naming the volume after her first story, *Naked, with Glasses,* it was awarded UKA Press' Grand Prize in its Annual International Writing Competition (2007).

The same dark humor, morally ambiguous subject matter, and sophisticated treatment found in her novels and poetry collections are present in her stories. Quirky characters abound. "BusMan," in the story of the same name, re-invents himself as a superhero after an unexpectedly frightening incident on his daily route.

Vincent, "Hunchback of the Midwest" and member of a traveling freak-show, regales his audience with tales of conquests over beautiful women, all the while longing for the one beauty he fears he will never possess.

Thirty years after the end of the violently protested 1960-70's "conflict," the Vietnam War comes to a small town's Convenience Store in the surprisingly affecting and disturbing "VC in the USA."

❀

Biblical characters populate many of the tales. Wandering in the Wilderness after escaping Pharaoh's enslavement in Egypt, the Hebrews begin to doubt their leaders, Moses and Aaron, as well as God Himself, in "Rebellion in the Promised Land."

Jesus, his followers, and the Romans who occupied Judaea during Jesus' lifetime frequently appear, involved in encounters not mentioned in biblical stories. "Passion Play" recounts Judas' and Mary Magdalene's attraction to and avoidance of each other, as they struggle with their mutual love for Jesus.

Sleepless and agitated, Roman Prefect Pontius Pilate is plagued by nightmares, doubts, and crumbling self-confidence after his unsettling encounter with Jesus in "Slaying the Dragon."

❀

As in Szeman's other work, the universal themes of family, love, loss, loyalty, and betrayal are visited in this collection as well. The narrator of "Me and Mom and JFK," now a grown man, recalls his childhood, when he competed with President Kennedy, before and after his assassination, for his own mother's love.

The spunky, unforgettable narrator of "St. Jerome Emiliani Comes to the Church Picnic" is reluctantly thrust into adulthood by a staggering "initiation."

Equally mournful and outraged, the mother of a suspected serial killer makes the rounds of TV talk-shows in "Midwestern

Madonna and Child," trying to explain why she's not to blame for whatever crimes her son's accused of, despite the media's incessant questions and insinuations.

Edgy, memorable, and engagingly written, these award-winning stories display another aspect of Szeman's talent — that for short fiction. Filled with distinct voices, unique characters, surprising plot-twists, and successful experimental writing innovations (such as "Sorry, Wrong Number, *Redux*," which is entirely in dialogue), this prize-winning collection secures the author's critically acclaimed reputation in this genre as well, adding to the accolades she has already garnered for her novels, poetry, and non-fiction.

Other Books by
Alexandria Constantinova Szeman

Novels

The Kommandant's Mistress, Revised & Expanded, 20th Anniversary Edition

Only with the Heart, Revised & Expanded, Legally & Medically Updated, 12th Anniversary Edition

No Feet in Heaven

The Kommandant's Mistress (1st Edition: HarperCollins 1993, 5 printings; HarperPerennial 1994, 4 printings; 2nd Edition [with translations of Verdi's opera *La Traviata*]: Arcade 2000, 6 printings), (formerly writing as "Sherri")

Only with the Heart (1st Edition: Arcade 2000, 8 printings), (formerly writing as "Sherri")

Short Stories

Naked, with Glasses

Poetry

Love in the Time of Dinosaurs

Where Lightning Strikes: Poems on the Holocaust

Creative Writing
Non-fiction

Mastering Point of View: Using POV and Fiction Elements to Create Conflict, Develop Characters, Revise Your Work, & Improve Your Craft, Revised, Updated, & Expanded, 12th Anniversary Edition

Mastering Point of View: How to Control POV to Create Conflict, Depth, & Suspense; (Story Press 2001, 4 printings), (formerly writing as "Sherri")

Naked,
with
Glasses

award-winning stories

*Alexandria
Constantinova
Szeman*
(formerly writing as "Sherri")

RockWay Press, LLC • New Mexico

Permissions & Publication Acknowledgments

Some of these stories have been published before (under different titles or in slightly different format, under the name "Sherri" Szeman) in the following journals and literary magazines:

Journals

• *Roanoke Review* (Roanoke College)
• *Soundings East* (Salem State College)
• *Tennessee Quarterly* (Belmont University)
• *Wisconsin Review*
• *Writers' Forum* (University of Colorado)

RockWay Press Trade Paper ISBN 9781940206998
LCCN 2012907383
E-Book ISBN 9780977663415

• Cover Artwork by Yurok (image #8093656), provided by 123RF (http://www.123RF.com), sister company of Inmagine (http://www.inmagine.com). Used with permission.

• Section divider designed by Francesco Abrignani (collection #12495781), provided by 123RF (http://www.123RF.com), sister company of Inmagine (http://www.inmagine.com). Used with permission.

• Cover design by Alexandria Szeman & RockWay Press, LLC. Copyright © 2012 Alexandria Szeman & RockWay Press, LLC.

• Interior design by RockWay Press, LLC. Copyright © 2013 Alexandria Szeman & RockWay Press, LLC.

• Author Photograph © 2013 by RockWay Press, LLC.

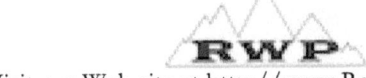

Visit our Web site at http://www.RockWayPress.com

for
Tom,

Home is not a place:
it is people.

L M Bujold

Acknowledgments

Grateful acknowledgment is made to the people who morally support me as I subject them to various literary genres. To my close friends — Becky Keller, Sharon Brown, Terrence Glass, Christopher Williams, and Evelyn Schott — who love me no matter how many times I switch genres on them.

To Andrea Lowne, Publisher of UKA [United Kingdom Authors] Press, who told me I could enter my short stories into their Annual International Contest (for critique purposes) as long as I understood that UKA Press had never published short stories and that I had no chance of winning the contest. Since I only wanted some feedback on the collection, I thank you for your honesty.

To all the outside readers/judges of UKA Press' Annual International Contest 2007 — all authors, editors, and publishers themselves — who gave me the best critique I could have ever gotten by awarding the manuscript the Grand Prize and insisting that UKA Press publish its first collection of short stories. Bless you all for your interest in my stories and in my other entries in your contests over the years. You are all honest, insightful, and thoughtful, and have provided me with invaluable feedback.

To Don Masters, my editor at UKA Press, whose excellent feedback on the stories helped me improve them while maintaining my own style and Voice: it takes an astute and sensitive editor to do so, Don, and I am grateful for all your wonderful suggestions. I am honored to be associated with UKA Press.

I also want to thank Andrea Lowne for allowing me to do the e-book version of *Naked, with Glasses* before UKA Press was ready to do the Trade Paper edition. Your professional grace and courtesy is part of what makes me honored to have my name still associated with your Press.

To Spike, Zoë, Vinnie, Hannah, Zeke, and Mosie: though you were taken from us far too soon, you're with us still. I thank you for your unconditional love as well as for lying on my desk and computer every single day while I wrote. I miss you more than I could ever say. You are in my heart forever.

To Shooter Tov, Mr. Eli, Trixie, Ling, Sascha, Sophie, and Sadie-Doggie: without having rescued you and brought you into our lives, my own happiness would be lessened. Thanks for letting me use my office, desk, printers, computer keyboard, and chairs when it doesn't inconvenience you too much. You know what you mean to me.

To Tom, with all my love: you know why.

Table of Contents

Author BIO, Photo, Amazon Page, Web-site, Twitter, Blog, & Contact Information

Naked,
with
Glasses

Part One

I will restore to you
the years the locust has eaten.

Joel 2:25

Naked, with Glasses

*T*his is how the plan to kill your husband could begin. You come home early from work. You have a headache. A terrible headache. The worst headache of your life. You have this grant proposal to write. It's not finished, and it was due yesterday. Your boss is gone for a week, so you bring the proposal home with you. After you open the door, you hear a noise.

"George?" you say.

Head throbbing, you wander into the living room. No one's there, but you hear another noise. Upstairs. You find your husband in the hallway which leads to the bedroom. He's naked, but he's wearing his glasses. To see you better. He's pale. He's sweating.

"George," you say, genuine concern in your voice, "what are you doing home in the middle of the day? Are you ill?"

He makes a movement, backward, toward the door. Too late. A young woman steps from the bedroom. She's also naked, but she's not wearing glasses. She doesn't have to: she can see you perfectly well. You can see her, too. She is young. Lovely. Thin. George introduces her.

"This is Monica," he says. "My assistant."

This is Monica. That is just like George. Naked, wearing glasses, saying to his wife, "This is my girlfriend." You say nothing. Your headache, however, suddenly gets worse. That is how the plan to kill your husband could begin.

Or perhaps it begins like this:

You and George go to the family reunion. It's his side of the family. It's hot. George's side of the family always insists on having reunions in the middle of July. In parks that have inadequate shelters. In parks that have no trees. George hates his family. He says this constantly.

"How I hate my family," he says. "Such a stupid family."

You hate his family, too. You, however, are not allowed to say this. Not to George. Not to your friends. Not even to yourself, alone, with no one else around. You aren't even allowed to think this. To think bad thoughts about George's family is bad. It's worse than a sin. It's worse than a crime. It's so bad, they haven't even invented a name for it yet. And George always knows when you're thinking bad thoughts about his family.

"Don't tell me you were trying to decide between the strawberry pie and the chocolate ice cream," he says. "I know perfectly well you were thinking how fat and ugly Great Aunt Mabel has gotten, and that I'm getting just like her."

You don't even remember which one *is* Great Aunt Mabel. They're all so fat and ugly, you can't keep them straight. That doesn't matter to George. He shoves both the ice cream and the pie off the concrete picnic table, into the grass. Everyone looks at him. The children cry. You look longingly at the knife.

There are no butcher knives at the picnic. After all, everyone eats sandwiches, cookies, snacks. They eat pie and ice cream. There's no food here for sharp knives. You think of sharp knives anyway. Long, sharp, glittering knives. Heavy-handled, glittering, butcher knives. You think of these beautiful sharp knives in connection with George. In connection with George's throat.

Or perhaps it starts like this:

You work late. On a project. It's important to you and to your company. It's important to your promotion. It's vital to your self-esteem. To your self-fulfillment. This project is not important to George. It annoys him. He doesn't like to cook his own dinner. He doesn't like you to cook his dinner the night before, and leave it for him to warm up. And he hates it when you come home, cook dinner, set it on the table for him, and go back to work. George hates that most of all. It means you're not a good wife.

He doesn't care about your education, your degrees, your career. He doesn't want to be liberated. He wants to be an old-fashioned man. A real man. He nags. He whines. He complains. He calls you every five minutes at work to ask questions. Stupid questions that a teacher shouldn't be asking. Questions like, "Where's the can opener?" or "What's it mean when the microwave goes *boom*?"

You discuss these things with Charles. Charles is your co-worker. He's writing the project with you. He sometimes answers the phone for you, so he recognizes George's voice. Charles tells George you're in the ladies' room.

He offers to take a message, but George says, "Never mind. It isn't important."

George doesn't call back the rest of the evening. You ask Charles to answer the phone every night for a week. He does. Charles is very understanding. He's a few years younger than you, but he doesn't act like it. He refuses to believe you when you tell him the year you were born. Charles is beautiful. When he leans forward over the desk, his hair falls over his forehead.

"How awful it must be for you," he says. "How dreadful."

You start to agree with this. Later, when Charles leans over the desk, your heart starts to pound. The office is air-conditioned, so it can't be the heat. When you get home at night, George is lying on the couch. Naked except for his glasses. Reading the newspaper. George isn't as young as Charles. He has no hair to fall over his forehead. He frowns at you, looks pointedly at the clock on the wall above the fireplace. His glasses glitter in the lamplight. His belly bulges under the paper. It is a decidedly un-pretty picture.

You think of Charles, his arms around you, his mouth open on yours. Naked, perhaps, but not wearing glasses. You decide killing George would be a pleasure. More than a pleasure. An absolute joy.

❀

Time passes. Life continues much in the same way. Much as everyone else's. Only worse. But you've changed. You've made a decision. You decide the ending will be different. You'll choose the ending to this life of yours. You. Nobody else.

❀

This is how it could end:

George and Monica think you've forgotten them. George says, "She means nothing to me." Monica doesn't get to say what she thinks of this remark. George weeps, falls on his knees, beats his breast, swears never to see her again. He swears on the Bible. He's very good at this. But George and Monica meet three afternoons a week. You know because you've been watching them. Your girlfriends and their children have been helping you. You haven't told this terrible story to your own children. No, that would upset them. But the others understand. They chart George's movements for you. They discover Monica's address, phone number, license plate, dress size. They discover that she has a fiancé. The fiancé's name is Michael. And Michael doesn't know about George.

So one of your friends calls the house. At 2:35 on Wednesday afternoon. 2:35 exactly. She's very prompt. You know because you're hiding in the kitchen. George and Monica don't know you're there, of course. They're too busy with each other. The phone rings. Right on schedule. Your friend says she's a nurse from the emergency room of the local hospital. She says she knows Monica's there because Monica's mother told her so. George gives the phone to Monica. What else can he do?

Your friend says, "I have terrible news for you, Monica."

Monica holds her breath. Standing in the kitchen, crouched near the doorway, you hold your breath, too.

Your friend says, "Your fiancé Michael has been in a motorcycle accident. A terrible motorcycle accident. One of the worst motorcycle accidents I've ever seen."

You know what she's saying because you wrote it yourself.

As a final touch, your friend says, "Your fiancé Michael wasn't wearing his helmet."

He does this sometimes. You know because some of the others have seen him do it. Monica knows it, too. She cries out. She drops the phone. She grabs her clothes and runs out of the house. George follows, but she's gone before he can get his clothes on. He stands in the doorway. Naked. Wearing his glasses. In the front doorway. Where everyone in the neighborhood can see him. He has no shame. You've suspected this for a long time, but now you know it for a fact.

You don't say anything to George as you come up behind him. You say absolutely nothing as you aim the gun. As you squeeze the trigger. George says nothing as he falls. His hands grasp at the empty air. His glasses shatter as his body hits the concrete of the front walk.

You smile. Your friends and the neighbor women gather around, nodding their approval. No one calls the police. There's no need to: the police chief's wife is your best friend. She's the one who gave you the gun.

✿

Or it could end like this:

You're packing your suitcase. Your heart is pounding and your face is flushed. You're so happy. George comes home. Your heart thuds. What's he doing home in the middle of the day? He comes into the bedroom. He looks at the suitcase. He looks around the room. The closets and bureau drawers are almost empty. The suitcase is filled with your clothes. George takes off his glasses, cleans them, puts them back on.

"What are you doing?" he says.

Charles is waiting for you at the airport, but you think it best not to tell George this. Not at this time. Not in this way. Besides, you've left a letter for him on his desk. You look at your watch. George stands in the doorway.

"Please let me go, George," you say.

"Not till you answer me," says George. "Not till you tell me exactly what's going on."

You try to push him aside but he's bigger than you. Heavier.

"Please, George," you say, "I'll explain everything to you later. But first I have to catch this plane."

George isn't listening to any of this. He walks in front of you as you go to the stairs. George is walking in front of you, but he's walking backward. So he can see you better.

"Tell me tell me tell me," he keeps saying.

You look at your watch. You should've been there long ago. What if Charles thinks you're not coming? You push George out of the way. A slight push. Against the chest. Not even a shove, really. You're a small woman and he's such a big man, after all. But he's standing at the top of the stairs. Right on the edge of the top step. Your push takes him by surprise. He falls. Backward. Down the whole flight of stairs.

His glasses glint in the light as his big body tumbles down the steps. His neck is broken.

It's not your fault. Everyone agrees about that. Of course, you'll have to change your flight. But Charles will understand.

Or perhaps it ends like this:

You're tired. It's been a long day. You know George didn't mean to ruin the microwave oven, but he's a teacher and you'd think that someone like that would know that you cannot put certain kinds of dishes into the oven.

George complains about his teaching assistant, whose name is Michael. Michael has a fiancée named Monica. George thinks Monica's a twit. She fell off her bicycle today and sprained her little finger. She called Michael away from the lab, just when George needed him. You don't care about Michael. You care even less for Monica, whom you've never met.

The proposal you wrote for the new project didn't get accepted. It didn't get rejected, but it didn't get accepted either.

"Let me think about this," your boss said. "Let me have Charles look it over."

Charles is younger than you. He's just graduated from college. You feel depressed. Angry. Hurt. Do you cry? Shout? Stomp your feet? No. You smile.

"That would be just fine," you say.

Charles is the boss' nephew.

Your head is throbbing by the time you get off work. You decide not to cook dinner. You'll warm up some food in the microwave. No, you'll try one of those new frozen meals that you just pop into the oven. You'll pour yourself a glass of wine, put your feet up, and relax. You smile, and your head starts to hurt a little less.

But when you get home, you find that George has broken the microwave. He didn't mean to, but he's not as smart as everyone else thinks he is. You throw something. Not at him, exactly. At the wall. He doesn't like how close the bowl comes to his head. You say three feet away isn't close. George doesn't agree. And after all, it's his head.

You run out of the house. You get into the car and drive away. You drive for hours. You think of all the terrible things you'll do to George. All the terrible, slow, painful things you'll do to George. To Charles. To your boss.

No: to yourself. Yes. that's it. You'll kill yourself. You'll deprive them of your existence. That'll show them.

You'll drive your car right over the edge of some cliff. A high, steep cliff, with jagged rocks and crashing waves at the bottom.

They'll find you at the last second. They'll beg you to hang on, just for one... more... minute. But it'll be too late. Oh, how they'll grieve. Oh, how they'll suffer. You drive and drive, looking for cliffs. You can't find any. That's because you live in Ohio. You curse yourself for moving with George to Ohio.

You think of an alternate plan to punish George and the rest of them. You'll drive into a tree. A big, old, oak tree. There are plenty of those in Ohio. They'll have to dig the car's twisted metal out of the tree. They'll have to use Jaws-of-Life to get you out of the twisted metal of the car. What's left of you will be almost unrecognizable. Except for your face, which will be untouched, and even more beautiful in death than it was in life. Yes. That'll show them. Oh, what weeping and wailing and gnashing of teeth. How they deserve it.

You drive and drive and drive, looking for just the right oak tree. You drive until you realize you're tired. Until you realize you're hungry. Then you go home.

❀

A cold dinner's sitting on the dining room table: salad, cheese, bread, wine.

There's a note from George.

"I'm sorry I ruined the microwave," it says.

You don't cry. You're too tired.

You go upstairs. George is in bed. He's lying on top of the covers, naked, reading student papers. He looks up when you come in. He puts down his pen and the student essays.

You sit on the side of the bed. You say nothing. Tears blur your vision. George takes off his glasses. Now his vision is the same as yours. He puts his hand on yours. Your fingers tighten.

This is how it could end.

Me & Mom & JFK

My mom was in love with John F. Kennedy. I'm pretty sure she never met him, and I know she didn't get the chance to vote for him since she was too young when he got elected, and he was assassinated before his first term was over. But she loved him more than anything else in the world.

I realized that the day he died. I was seven years old, in school, trying to make the letters in my spelling words straighter, so I wouldn't have to do them over tomorrow, when the intercom buzzed.

The principal's voice came on. She was crying. Sister Mary Margaret, crying over the intercom in school. Everyone knew it had to be something bad, even David O'Donovan. We all sat there, still as death, David O'Donovan included, and listened as Sister Mary Margaret sobbed over the intercom.

"The President... He's been shot. President Kennedy's... dead."

Before any of us had a chance to say anything, Sister Mary Thomas started to cry in the front of class. None of us laughed, not even Eddie Madison. We sat there and looked at each other. We never even knew that the Sisters were sisters, let alone that they had a brother who was the President. We were so stunned by the Sisters Mary crying in class that nobody was surprised when Sister Mary Margaret announced that school was dismissed for the rest of the day. We all got up real quiet, went to our lockers, and left without hitting each other on the back with chalk-dust-covered erasers, or shooting spitballs out of straws stolen from the cafeteria during lunch, or pulling the girls' hair, or anything.

Walking home, me and Eddie Madison kept talking about President Kennedy and how he'd got shot. Spanky Morrison and his twin brother Mouth were older, and usually they wouldn't even beat us up 'cause we weren't worth noticing, but they walked home with me and Eddie the day the President died. Spanky Morrison wondered how many times he'd been shot, with what kind of gun, and where he'd been hit. Mouth volunteered to find whoever'd done it and beat the daylights out of him. Me and Eddie wished we could do something, too. I could hardly wait to get home and tell Mom. She wouldn't believe what had happened. The sun was shining bright, but it was pretty cold that day.

I left Eddie and Spanky and Mouth at the corner and raced up to our house to tell Mom that the Sisters Mary had a brother named John and that he'd been shot dead. But the television was already on the news, real loud, with Mom sitting in front of it, crying.

I stopped. The news reporter was talking about President Kennedy's death. The reporter was crying, too. I sat down on the footstool, and was real careful not to make any sound. I looked at the television when they showed a picture of the President. He was young, too young to die on his own. Kinda like my dad, who I didn't remember hardly at all. I shivered. Mom was crying so much, I don't think she noticed I was home from school.

They showed nothing but the President all day, and one of the reporters used his hand and his pen to show where President Kennedy had been shot. They didn't have any pictures of the bullets, but they did have some of the blood. Mom cried so loud that I had to pretend I wasn't looking when those pictures came on.

After a while, I went into the bedroom and sat on the bed with the door open, listening to Mom cry. When the neighbors came in, crying as hard as Mom, I picked up my baseball, tossed it up almost to the ceiling, and caught it over and over and over again.

Eddie dropped by later and said his mom and his sisters were crying their eyes out, too. Eddie and me sat in the basement till late. We didn't even feel like tossing the ball or crushing the spiders in the corners or making prank phone calls or nothing.

Afterwards, when the television showed all the people lining the streets, sobbing and crying as the President's flag-draped casket slowly passed by, I felt like something got caught in my throat, and I knew the President's death was the worst thing that could have happened to the world.

Nobody had to tell me it would change everything.

I knew.

People set couches on fire in the streets. They threw empty beer bottles at cars and house windows; they stole kids' bikes and knocked out all the spokes in the wheels before leaving them a few blocks away. Mom and me lived near the college, and one night when we were trying to get home from the grocery, we turned onto our street and saw first-hand how everything was turned upside-down.

Couches and cars were burning in the street, college students were screaming and pounding on cars, police were sitting on the curbs with blood running down their faces. The college kids surrounded Old Man Jackson's car and rocked it back and forth until it tipped over; then they started jumping up and down, cheering and shrieking.

"Roll up the windows, quick," said Mom, and I did.

I got down on the floor in the back seat, my slingshot ready. As soon as one of them started rocking our car, *Bammo:* I'd let him have it good. The college kids slammed their hands against the windows, and pounded their fists on the roof, hood, and trunk. Their mouths screamed, and their eyes were filled with something I'd never seen before. I wanted to fire my rocks right into those eyes, while, all around us, the fires burned.

"If Kennedy was alive, he'd fix them," said Mom. "Just like the Russians in Cuba."

After we made it home, we bolted the doors. Me and my slingshot offered to keep watch on the front porch, in case anybody tried to break in and set fire to our couch, but Mom said it'd be better if we guarded her from my room upstairs. We kept the lights turned off so no one could see us, and Mom peeked out between the curtains.

"Kennedy wouldn't let them run loose on the streets," she said. "He'd show 'em who's boss."

But President Kennedy wasn't there to show them who was boss, so things got worse. At colleges all over the country, students screamed and burnt things, and nobody seemed to be able to make them stop. Every day on the playground Eddie Madison said he was going to be just like those college kids when he grew up, but none of us believed it because none of us thought we'd grow up. We thought the world would end, any day, since now that President Kennedy was dead, no one was left who'd be able to stop it. At night, I lay awake in my bed and prayed that the world wouldn't blow up into a fireball.

I prayed the war in Vietnam that killed Eddie's big brother would end before Eddie and me had to be soldiers. I prayed that President John F. Kennedy would come back from the dead to make my mom stop crying, to make everything the way it was supposed to be, but Kennedy didn't come back, even for a day. Mom cut out all the pictures of John F. Kennedy that she found in the *Life* magazines, and hung the pictures on the living room wall. Every night while we watched the news, Mom would glance up at President Kennedy, to make sure he was getting it all, but he never gave any sign when I was in the room.

"He'd fix things," said Mom, "if he was here."

I guess that was one of the reasons Mom loved him.

☙

Soon most of the pictures on the wall faded, on account of the sun shining right through the window, and Mom blamed herself for not framing the pictures and covering them with glass. Every time I found a new picture of President Kennedy, I brought it home, and as she smiled at the picture, she'd run her fingers through my hair. It made me feel good to bring those pictures home. Like I was doing something to keep the world safe.

Then one day, Mom came home with something bulky and heavy, wrapped in newspaper, tied with string. She had a big smile on her face as she unwrapped it. Layer after layer of newspaper fell away until, finally, I saw it: a life-sized head of President John F. Kennedy. I thought the statue looked just like him, and I said so, but Mom said it wasn't a statue: it was a bust. I didn't know how that could be, since he wasn't a girl, but Mom looked so happy, I couldn't bear to say anything to her about it.

She put the head of John F. Kennedy on the coffee table, then she sat down on the couch and looked at him the whole night, with tears in her eyes. That's when I knew what real love was: when it's real love, you don't even need the actual person there. Just his head's enough to bring that look to your face.

President Kennedy's head stayed on our coffee table for a long time, for years, until one terrible day, the day me and Eddie did something I've never forgiven myself for, the day I destroyed my mother's life.

That Saturday started out like usual. Mom went to work at the grocery, while I stayed on the couch in my pajamas watching cartoons on television. Even though I wasn't a kid anymore, sometimes I liked to watch cartoons just for fun.

Around 11:00, Eddie came over. We watched "Mighty Mouse" for a while, then we started talking about who was better, Underdog or Mighty Mouse. Of course, Eddie said it couldn't be Mighty Mouse, because he was only a mouse, but I thought there could be some advantages to being small: you could get into places that a dog couldn't. Then Eddie said that was because I was a shrimp myself, so I had to ball up my socks and throw them at his head. Eddie threw the socks back, and they hit me, real hard, in the eye. That made me mad, so I punched him. Then Eddie did his soldier yell and landed on me. I had to start kicking to save myself. Eddie yelled and smashed me, my foot kicked out and hit the coffee table, and then President Kennedy's head wobbled, teetered, and crashed to the floor.

Me and Eddie were off that couch in a second.

"God-dog-it," I said.

We looked at each other a minute or two before we scrambled over the coffee table to the fractured head. We were afraid to touch it. I mean, I wasn't even allowed to dust it, Mom was so worried something would happen to it, and now, look what we'd done to the President.

"Mom's going to kill me."

"Maybe she won't notice."

"I'm dead."

"Yep."

We stared at it a couple more seconds before I started to pick up the pieces of President Kennedy's head.

"Let's see if we can make it stand up on its own," said Eddie. "Maybe your mom won't notice he's broken."

Kennedy's head wouldn't stand up on its own, and the third time Eddie tried, Kennedy's hair slid off his head and broke into even more pieces.

"Double-God-dog-it," said Eddie. "I'm outta here."

The door banged behind Eddie, and while I stood there, feeling sick and trying to figure out a plan, President Kennedy's face just stared at me. Finally I decided the only thing I could do was move him out of the living room so he wouldn't be the first thing Mom saw when she came in from work. I took the President's hair and face and shoulders into the kitchen, and carefully put them on the table. I wasn't even going to try to put his head back together: I was too nervous about getting more of him broken.

I stared at him a while, then went over to the sink and washed my cereal bowl and spoon. Then I washed the spaghetti plates and pan from last night's supper. I wiped off the countertops, the stove, and the table. I scoured out the sinks with cleanser. After I did the kitchen, I raced upstairs and gathered all the wet towels in the bathroom to put them in the hamper. I picked up all of my room, and I mean all of it. I didn't just shove things under the bed, either: I put them away in the closet, in my toy-chest, and in my drawers. I even went into Mom's room and made her bed before I went downstairs. I was running the vacuum in the living room, picking up the last powdery bits of President Kennedy's hair, when Mom came home.

"Wow, Kenny," she said. "What's gotten into you?"

As soon as she kicked off her shoes and collapsed on the couch, she saw what was missing. She didn't say anything: she only looked at me. I knew it was going to kill me, to show her the President, but it wasn't like I could hide it from her. With my head bent down real low, staring at the ground all the way into the kitchen, I led her to President Kennedy.

The sound she made when she saw him scared me. I thought maybe she was going to die herself. I thought she might kill me. When she sat down at the table, her fingers moved real slow over the President's hair, his nose, his mouth. His eyes stared up at the ceiling. Mom stared at him.

She didn't look at me. She gathered up President Kennedy's hair and face, and she tried to make them sit on his shoulders again, like Eddie had done before. They wouldn't stay put for Mom either.

After the second time they fell off, she reached out her arms and swept all of President Kennedy's face and hair and neck and shoulders against her chest. She bent her head over the broken President and cried. I realized then how much Mom loved John F. Kennedy. I'd never seen her cry like that: not when Grandma died, not when she lost her job as manager at the cleaners and had to go work as a cashier at the grocery, not even when my dad left for cigarettes and never came back. She cried even harder than all those times put together, the day I killed President John F. Kennedy. Again.

❀

Kennedy never come back, yet the world didn't explode or consume itself in fire. I grew up without losing too many teeth in fistfights, wore out jeans faster than Mom could buy me new ones, got a paper route, and saved all my money for a new bike.

The war that killed Eddie's big brother and the Morrison twins ended before me or Eddie had to go. The only thing students were protesting by the time I went to college was the choice of soft drinks in the cafeteria. The first two years I went to the college near Mom's house, but when Pam transferred to law school, Mom encouraged me to follow.

Mom stood up for me at the wedding, and she cried when we named the twins Jackie and John. Pam found a beautiful print of President Kennedy and gave it to Mom on the twentieth anniversary of his death. The three of us held hands as we sat on the couch at Mom's house watching the retrospective on John F. Kennedy, and none of us was wiped away the tears on our faces.

Somehow I grew up and the world survived without President Kennedy, but I never forgave myself for killing him a second time. Mom never said a word about it, but it's been a hard thing to live with, all these years, and I always vowed that if I could ever find a way to make it up to Mom, I would.

❀

Last year, in a South Dakota gift shop, I found John F. Kennedy's head. It was almost exactly the same as the one I'd destroyed so many years ago. I bought it. The clerk wrapped it up in newspaper and bubble-wrap before she put it in a box, so it wouldn't get broken on the flight home. I guarded the President's head as carefully as if I were a Secret Service agent assigned to protect him.

I didn't even stop at the apartment. I went straight to Mom.

It was late. Too cold for anyone else to be out. Twilight. I stood in front of Mom, and, without saying a thing, opened the box with my pocketknife, cut open the bubble-wrap and the newspaper, and offered President Kennedy to her. She didn't have to say anything. I could feel her joy.

I knelt down, swept away the snow, and carefully set down President Kennedy. It felt good, doing that for Mom. I liked the way President Kennedy's head looked, dark and solemn against the white of the snow, dark and solemn against the light grey of the headstone. I stayed with Mom a long time, till after dark. It made me happy to have all of us back together again.

Me and Mom and JFK.

Helena, of the *Sangre de Christo* Mountains

*T*here are lines right through these mountains, where glaciers have gouged into them and the railroad has blasted through. There are lines in the mountains and lines in the desert, too, and there were lines in her face. Out here, lines are a natural part of the landscape. She was part of that land — faded, isolated, rugged, tough — in a word: beautiful. I loved her from the moment I saw her.

I wasn't born or raised in this country, but I'd been in the asphalt fields of Manhattan and the verdant fields of Modesto, and when I saw New Mexico, it was like the hand of God came down from the heavens and pushed me to it. My train ticket was a straight path to Chicago coming back from the west coast, but that New Mexico landscape ripped me and my duffel bag right off that train.

New Year's Eve. Not a snowflake in sight. All the land parched and dull brown. Still, I stood there after the train slid away thinking, "At last, I've found it."

❁

It wasn't too hard to get a job, though they didn't believe I'd been around horses till I showed them, and I had to change my khakis and loafers for jeans and boots. I took the hardest, loneliest jobs I could get, working my way further south with every one, away from the few big cities. To be with those mountains, those buttes, those high deserts covered with juniper, piñon, prickly pear, and cholla. I was content sleeping out under the stars, drinking bitter coffee by the campfire, talking to nobody but my horse and the mountains and God. By the time I reached the *Sangre de Christo* Mountains, I knew I'd found my home.

Then I saw her.

She was mending barbed wire at the end of her ranch. Her hands were quick and sure. She wasn't the type of woman I was attracted to, but I loved her the moment I saw her. She was lean and hard, no breasts or buttocks, but those hands of hers moved like dry lightning. I was bull-dogged in an instant. When she looked up — that face was like nothing I'd ever seen. I was drawn to her like to water in the desert.

"You must be Parris," she said when I rode up. "Everyone says you ain't bad for a city-boy."

"Ain't been a city-boy for years now."

"Lemme see your hands," she said, and I pulled off my gloves.

After she nodded, I dismounted to watch her work, but she didn't look at me anymore, and she kept quiet. I couldn't stop staring at her face.

"So, how'd you get a name like Parris?" she finally said. "Your folks watch too many movies, or you make it up yourself?"

My face burned red. My tongue was dry in my mouth.

"I thought so."

She smiled.

"Parris ain't something you'd even name a dog or a horse unless you was too rich to have to work for a living. Or unless you want to be an actor. Still, you kinda look like a Parris."

"Want help with the fence?"

She handed me a pair of wire-cutters. We worked all morning, the wire flashing in the sun, her teeth flashing, my heart lunging every time she looked at me. We worked without talking.

Around noon, she pushed her hat back, and the wind tugged her sun-whitened hair. She yanked off her gloves, poured some water into her hand, and splashed the liquid onto her face.

"Lunch time," she said.

She pulled her pack off her horse, and I followed her over to a juniper. She spread the lunch on the ground: bread, coffee, hard cheese, grapes, and an apple. With a knife from her belt-loop she halved the apple and held it out, then stood waiting for me to take the fruit. When I held out my hands, she gasped, then frowned at me.

"Why didn't you tell me you cut yourself?"

"It's nothing. A scratch."

"Still, you don't want to get any dirt in that."

The sun glowed on her skin and hair as she dampened her handkerchief and wiped my palm clean.

"What's your name?" I said, my voice hoarse.

"My name's not as pretty as yours," she said, handing me a cloth to dry my hand as she picked up the fruit again. "You better make one up for me."

I looked at her face and saw the jagged uneven lines of the mountains, split cracked valleys, red rocks and boulders piled into buttes by years of avalanches, arroyos gouged out by melted snows and monsoons, sagebrush and cholla clinging to sandy soil that swirls away in great dust-storms, snow on mountain-tops, blue-grey clouds heavy with rain that never falls on the parched earth, and a rose-blue sky in the sunset.

I reached out my hand and touched a drop of moisture sparkling near her mouth. She jerked away, blushed, dropped the apple, smoothed her hair. Her wedding band glinted gold in the sun.

"Fairest of the fair," I said. "Come: make me immortal with a kiss."

St Jerome Emiliani Comes to the Church Picnic

When I was little, Mama and Daddy tole me nobody but old folks died. Before I was even growed, I found out my Mama and Daddy lied. Anybody cain die. Even folks young as me. Folks cain die right smack in the middle a playing with they doll babies, right smack in the middle a eating mashed potatoes at supper, right smack in the middle a Saturday night bath. Folks cain die right smack in the middle a anything at all. Ain't no way to stop it neither.

The day I found out my Mama and Daddy done lied to me was the day of the church picnic. Mama done went off early in the morning, to be with her pies and her lady friends. Daddy carried us there later, just before lunch. He pulled right up to the front gate, and give us each a quarter.

"Y'all get on out now," he says. "Go say 'Hey' to the Reverend. I'll be in directly."

Annabelle Lee and Clyde Junior they just jumps right outta the car, before he even finishes talking. You sure cain tell they's twins. Even though they's boy and girl, they's identical selfish. To the very bone. My own self, I am more polite. I waits till he finishes before I opens the door.

'Course Annabelle Lee and Clyde Junior don't pay him no never mind. They's already at the gate, jumping up and down in fronta the preacher, almost wetting they own selves in they excitement. I act more dignified. More growed-up. Lotsa folks is pushing through the gate. Some of them boys 'bout run me down, and don't even say 'scuse me neither: they's just like the twins. Lotsa folks knows Mama and Daddy, and they all says, "Hey."

"Hey, MaryLouise, where's your Ma?"

"Over at the pies."

"Where's your Pa, MaryLouise?"

"Parking the car."

21

"Where's your Ma?"

"At the pies."

"Where's your Pa?"

"Parking the car."

After 'bout three-billion-trillion "parking the car's," I starts to wonder what in tarnation is taking Daddy so long. Don't take that long to park no car, even if it is a big brand new one that he parks real far from all the resta the cars so it don't get no dings nor dents nor scratches in its brand spanking new $25 paint job. Annabelle Lee and Clyde Junior starts in whining and crying like dogs got they tails stepped on, and says they gotta go find Mama.

"Don't you be going nowheres," I says. "Daddy done tole us to wait by the front gate."

They turns up they ugly little twin faces at me, and squinches they ugly little twin eyes.

"We going over to be with our own Mama," they says.

And they runs theyselves off before I cain even grab aholt of they collars. 'Course they don't come back. Didn't I tell you they's selfish? Ain't got no respect, them two. Why if I'd done that kinda disrespecting when I was they age, I'd been whupped for certain. Them, they'll probably get no more'n a mean look and a "I tole you two don't you do that no more." But you cain bet that ain't gonna stop them two none.

After a while, I get kinda tired of waiting on Daddy.

"How long's it take to park a car?" I asks my own self, and I decide it don't take near as long as he's been gone. I reckon I best go look for him and fetch him into the church yard.

The parking lot is little rocks in some places and dried-up grass in others. Daddy didn't tell us where he's gonna park, so I gotta look up and down, up and down, up and down every row. There's lotsa cars here today, I cain tell you. I ain't never seen so many cars in one place in all my life. I keeps on walking, looking for the car. Sometimes I am walking in dried-up grass. Sometimes I am walking on little rocks. It is fun to throw these little rocks. They's just the right size for throwing. Wait: I ain't here to throw no little rocks. I am looking for my Daddy. I drop them little rocks.

Finally I finds the car. Daddy ain't there, but the door is open. Now this is mighty particular. Daddy don't never go nowhere away from the car and leave the door open. I figures he gotta be standing somewhere, jawing with the fellas, but I sure ain't seeing him nowheres.

I reckon he done forgot about us standing by the front gate like he done tole us to his very own self. I reckon by this much time past he's over to the pies where Mama is. 'Course Annabelle Lee and Clyde Junior done tole him by now how *I* was the one who run off and left *them* by they own selves so they was *forced* to come find Mama so they'd not be all alone just the two of them just them two little twins all by they own selves in the middle of the church picnic all by they lonesomes. I cain just hear it now. I closes the car door, drags my feet, kicks at some of them little rocks that is so nice for throwing, and walks my self on back to the church yard gate.

❀

All a sudden, folks is running. Men-folk mostly, but some women-folk, too. Running past me, in the direction I just come from. Funny looks on they chalk-pale faces. So I runs, too.

They runs they selves back toward the very furtherest side of the church parking lot. Where it is all grass, and none of them little rocks at all. They's all running to the little boys' room. And they's all going right in, too, all of them: they just running they selves right in to the little boys' room. Even the girls and the growed women who I knows cain read. So I goes on in, too.

Right away, sure as I'm born, without nobody saying nuthin at all to me, I knows something powerful bad's done happened. The looks on they faces is something awful. And it's real quiet in there. But it ain't quiet like church-quiet come Sunday morning. No, it ain't like that. It's bad-quiet. Some of the women-folk is shaking they heads. They got they hands over they mouths. In they hands which is over they mouths, they got they flower-stitched handkerchiefs. The men-folk is shaking they heads, too. They's talking real low to they selves. And everybody that done run they selves over here is all standing in front of this here one stall.

One of the more growed boys wearing tore overalls is holding the door open. So everybody cain look right in. Now that don't seem at all right to me, but then Mama and Daddy done always tole me I ain't even *allowed* to go into the little boys' room, but here I am, clear as daylight, nobody not a single person on God's green earth stopping me. That's 'cause they's all too busy with they eyes looking in the stall where the boy in the tore overalls is holding open the door. So I looks, too.

You cain knock me over with a chicken feather. You cain knock me over with the breath outta you mouth. You cain knock me over without nuthin at all. What they was all looking at was a man.

A growed man was there, with his pants full on, kneeling on the floor, his backside sticking out at all of us, his head down in the toilet. For the life of me I cain't figure what he's doing like that. 'Specially with everybody in the whole entire world in the universe standing there gawking at him. Don't he hear all of us? Don't he notice that the door is being held wide open?

"He's dead," says one of the men-folk to another.

"You reckon?"

"Like a doornail."

"How can y'all be so disrespectful?"

"Shouldn't we do something?"

"Sheriff's on his way."

"Cain't we at least lay him down?"

All the men-folk looks at each other but nobody moves.

Nobody moves 'cepting me, and I am staring at the patch on the back of the man's jeans. It's a blue patch. Blue with little white stars on it. Blue with little white stars in the shape of hearts. Blue with little white stars in the shape of hearts from my old jumper that I am too growed to wear anymore and which Annabelle Lee cut on with a scissors because she is such a stupid selfish little twin. The blue patch with the little white stars in the shape of a heart is on the back of the man's jeans.

That man is my Daddy.

'Course I don't say nuthin to nobody. I cain't say nuthin to nobody even if I was to try. My mouth's hanging open and all, but no words is coming out. No words is coming outta my mouth which is open to the ground, but them words is in my brain all right. And them words is running 'round and 'round and 'round, bashing into my head bones, and them words is saying, "No, no, only old folks die."

But my Daddy is in the little boys' room on the other side of the parking lot at the church picnic. My own Daddy is kneeling on the floor with his head stuck in the toilet and some boy with tore overalls is holding the door wide open so everybody and his brother cain see and all the folks is standing 'round shaking they heads and whispering "how sad how awful dreadful sad" while my own Daddy is kneeling there not moving nary a little finger and I my own self am standing there with my mouth hung open wide enough for a bird to build its self a nest in not saying no word not no single word at all.

I reckon it must be for a fact, what they been saying about him being dead.

❁

When Mama gets her self there, she screams and starts to crying. Then somebody gets to noticing that *children* is in the little boys' room, and some of them children is little *girls,* and one of them children which is little girls is *me.*

"Oh, my God, oh, sweet baby Jesus," they says as they kinda push-pulls me out of the little boys' room, out into the parking lot where the grass is all tramped down from all the folks running they selves over here, out where the dried-up grass turns its brown self into them little rocks which is just the right size for throwing, out where the sun is shining hot enough to fry a egg without no skillet.

But I cain't feel nuthin. Not even the sun beating down on my head.

I cain't see nuthin neither. 'Cept that little blue patch with white stars in the shape of a heart.

And I cain't hear nuthin 'cept big words and Mama crying hard enough to choke her self and Annabelle Lee and Clyde Junior crying even harder till somebody finally done picks the twins up and takes them over to a neighbor's house which is nearby the church yard.

I cain't hear nuthin but weeping and wailing and growed doctor words like "mass-of-corn-airy" and "corn-airy-fail-your" and "They's St. Jerome Miliani's widow and orphans now," but they all means the same thing.

Dead.

And dead means forever. Dead means forever and ever till the end of the world. Dead means no cake on your birthday with one more candle than you done had last year, and no powder-smelling

Mama to kiss both your cheeks and your forehead at night so's you can sleep with pretty pictures, and no rides up to your own warm bed at night on Daddy's shoulders, the Daddy you love more'n anything else in the whole wide world around and who you want to marry your own self when you's all growed up.

Dead means till Jesus his own sweet self comes back to raise you up from the ground where you's laid for hundreds or thousands of years and takes your sweet lonely old bones up to heaven to match them with your skin. Dead means darkness and coldness and shivering and loneliness. Dead means never ever again. Dead means nuthin at all for the rest of your whole entire life on earth.

Dead means you done found out your very own Daddy lied to you.

'Course, I coulda forgive him for that.

But he ain't never give me no chance to.

Part Two

All animals are equal,
but some ... are more equal than others.

George Orwell
Animal Farm

Midwestern Madonna and Child

*T*hey was born on the same day, less than a minute apart, but those two boys wasn't nothing alike. Nicky — now there was an angel, straight from heaven, he was. But you don't want to hear about Nick. No, nobody wants to hear about the good son I raised. Nobody from them talk shows calls up to hear about my good son, Nick. Everybody wants to talk about the bad boy — and they all want to blame everything on me.

But how about that dog, huh? What about it? Like how I never believed Frank found it in the first place. He probably stole it from some neighbor's yard and took the tags off so nobody'd know. This sweet little puppy — the sweetest, happiest, friendliest puppy you ever did see — I tell you, my Nick was just crazy about that puppy. He adored that little dog. And Frankie knew it. One day Nicky's out back petting the dog and playing catch and being all happy, and next thing you know, the dog's gone. Frank's gone, too.

Nick's going all over the yard, front and back, calling, "Pepper, Pepper," but we can't find the dog anywhere. Soon all the neighbor boys and girls are looking, everybody calling, "Pepper, Pepper."

Frank ain't calling. In fact, nobody's seen hide nor hair of Frankie in ever so long. Then all the sudden, who strolls down the street and into the yard? You guessed that right.

"Frank, you seen Pepper?"

He just shakes his head real innocent.

"Pepper's gone?" he says.

Poor Nick. He cries all night long.

Next morning, Frank gets outta bed and says, real casual, "I think I figured out where Pepper might be."

He takes Nicky to find him. A couple hours later, Nicky comes flying back, by himself this time — his T-shirt and jeans torn, nose bleeding.

He's crying so hard, he can't see where he's going, and real loud he's saying, "He ain't my brother no more, I ain't never playing with him again, I hate him, I hate him."

"What happened, Baby? Tell Mama."

Nicky turns around, his little face messed up with blood and dirt, and he says, "Pepper's dead."

He locks himself in his room. I can't get him to open for nothing nor nobody, even me. Then Frank comes home.

"What'd you do to Pepper?"

"I found him. In the woods."

Then I grab him by the collar on accounta he's just gonna walk away from me, and I say, "What'd you do?"

Nicky yells from the top of the stairs, "He killed Pepper. He tied a rope around his neck, and he hanged him in a tree."

It was all I could do to keep Nicky from throwing himself on Frankie again and getting beat up worse than he already was. Though they're twins, Frankie was always the bigger. Yeah, Frank was always bad news, even when he was just a kid.

You heard what he done to that little Johnson boy, didn't you? Yeah, when he took him out to the garage, locked the door, and was teaching him how to smoke. Ain't never heard of nobody getting cigarette burns all over his back and legs learning how to smoke. I know that Johnson boy said he kept dropping the cigarette himself, and that he bought the cigarettes in the first place, and that Frank didn't have nothing to do with it, but you think I believe that? Nick was there in the garage with them, but he'll tell you the same thing if you was to ask him.

What about that girl, Aimee? You know: the one who said he done things no self-respecting boy'd do to a girl, even if she wanted him to. Why those things are wrote out in the Bible itself as being damned. The police said they couldn't prosecute on accounta there wasn't enough evidence that a crime had been committed. Nobody wanted to listen to what Nicky said, though he was a eye-witness — they said since he was Frank's brother, and his twin at that, he couldn't no way be impartial. But I always wondered about what that girl said.

I did too punish him. I made Frank stay in the basement for a few weeks to pray and think on what he done, even if the girl had said *yes* like he claimed, 'cause the Bible condemns it either way. That girl? She went downhill fast — smoking, drinking, cursing, having babies without being married, getting beat up night after night by whatever guy she was with. Maybe Frankie did do something to that girl that he shouldn't oughta done. That don't make it my fault.

And the things they're saying about him now. Who could believe any of that, I ask you? No red-blooded American boy could do that to another human being, and to pretty young girls besides.

'Course, I know *somebody* must be doing it. I listen to the news. I seen the pictures. I'm saying it ain't Frankie. Not the boy I carried in my own body for nine months along with his sweet angel brother Nicky.

No, he didn't do it. He didn't. 'Cause I say so. All right, let's pretend. It's your show. Even if he did do it — which he didn't — it ain't my fault.

I loved that boy, every day, as hard as I could, as much as I could, I taught him right from wrong, just like I did his twin brother Nicky. I ain't no mother like the kind they got nowadays — off to work and not caring where her boys are or what they're doing. Latch-key kids? I don't know what that is. All I know is, I watched my boys, trained 'em to grow up right, in fear of the Lord.

Some of those poor girls — "unrecognizable," that's what the police said, buried all over different places. FBI wants to dig up my backyard. That's what they told me last night on the phone. They think some little girl from Memphis could be there.

No, trust me: there ain't no body in our backyard. No cat, no dog, no bird, and definitely not no girl down from Memphis who was visiting her aunt and disappeared after she met a couple boys at some party who resembled Frank and Nicky. Those police and FBI can dig and dig all day long, they ain't gonna find nothing.

There ain't no skeletons in my backyard.

Ain't none in my closets, neither.

BusMan

*T*hey lied when they said I killed my mother, but that didn't stop Betty from leaving me and taking the kids. She even flipped me off after she slammed the car door. Yeah, like I believed they were my kids in the first place. She was probably having an affair with Mr. Ft.-Wayne-Detective-of-the-Year, and I'll bet he was proud of himself after he hounded me out of my job. But I don't give a damn about them anymore.

I got a new face, a new name, a new life. They can't touch me here because they don't know where I am. Hell, I don't even know where I am — some godforsaken place surrounded by cornfields, and populated by cows that got more brains than the local broads. I light up a cigarette and drive to the first stop on my shift.

Nobody's there. It starts to rain. I pull my paperback from above the visor and lean back to enjoy my cigarette. Halfway through Raskolnikov's first job, some guy in a suit taps on the door of the bus. He's holding a newspaper over his head, but Raskolnikov's just been caught in the act by the demented sister, so I pretend I don't hear Mr. Suit hit the doors harder and yell about the rain. He keeps on pounding. *Jesus H. Christ.* I pull the lever so the doors *whoosh* open. Mr. Suit glares at his fancy gold watch and stares at me. He drops his token in.

My foot slips off the airbrake, and I have to slam it down real hard so nobody boarding gets hurt. Despite my quick reflexes, Mr. Suit and his briefcase are thrown back down the steps into Bag Lady. She lets out a big toothless laugh and clamps her arms around him. Probably a long time since she had any. She smacks her big lips and coos real romantic-like. Suit whips out a handkerchief and wipes himself and his briefcase as he staggers to a seat. Serves him right. These glasses are a disguise, not an indication of my IQ. Bag Lady doesn't pretend to put any tokens in, but as long as she doesn't grab my thigh again, I could care less.

The little missy behind Bag Lady is wearing fishnet tights with holes big enough for mackerel to swim through, and a skirt so short it doesn't cover her navel. She digs around in a beaded carpetbag like she's looking for change. I flick something off my pants leg, take a real slow drag on my cigarette, and watch the rain on the windshield. Fried Brains pushes up against Miss Fishnet, loses his balance when she shoves him away, and ends up halfway down the steps with his face on my name plate.

He blinks a couple times, but my new name's got more letters in it than he ever learned. Finally he leans on the pole beside Miss Fishnet and drools. She shakes her head and looks up at me with one of those looks like Flo used to give me after I'd been playing a little poker with the boys all night.

"You got any change, Mister?" Fishnet says. "I forgot my change purse."

Yeah, yeah, yeah, and hell froze over when I wasn't looking, and pigs got pilots' licenses now, and I used to knock that look off Flo's face. If I give a woman money, it ain't so she can ride no bus. I don't care what kind of look Miss Fishnet gives me, and I don't care if it *is* pouring outside.

After she gets off the bus, I wrench the wheel away, splashing mud and grimy water so next time she won't yank my chain. The bus lurches into a pothole, and Fried Brains yells *Hey* just before he falls into Suit. Bag Lady claps like she's at the damn theater.

❁

The next three stops are empty, and all the time I'm driving, I'm thinking about my man Raskolnikov. Is he going to get caught or isn't he? Is he going to do somebody else, or isn't he? Is he going to get sent to one of those Gulags in Siberia, where I'd send Betty and Mr. Ft.-Wayne-Detective-of-the-Year if they ever found me...

Suddenly Suit yells. In the mirror, I see him shove Fried Brains away. Bag Lady goes into her applause routine, then stops real quick when Fried Brains twirls and points at her. *Jesus F. Christ.* Fried Brains has a gun. I shout while looking in the rear-view mirror.

"Hey. Hey, Boy."

Boom. Out goes one of the windows. Bag Lady screams and claps her hands over her ears. Suit disappears under one of the seats, and no one else is on the bus. I slam on the brakes and yank the wheel hard left then right so the gun flies out of Fried Brains' hand and slides up the center aisle. I slam the bus into *park,* snatch up the pistol, and shove the muzzle against his temple before he can get up off his hands and knees.

I'm guessing he didn't think I could move that fast. Yeah, I've surprised people all my life. So, he's down on his knees, and his hands are folded like he's praying. He whimpers something about Mama, like anybody cares about his Mama. Snot and tears run over his face. I tell him to shut up. He blubbers on. I bash him in the head with the gun.

"Not on my bus," I say.

I yank him up by his dirty collar and drag him to the front of the bus.

He flies out those bus doors like he's on the best drug of his life. I turn around. Bag Lady looks at me like I'm the Christ or the Anti-Christ, she can't decide which, and her hands clutch the seat in front like it's the Rapture and she's afraid she's going to be left behind. Suit reappears, brushes himself off, but stops when he sees me looking. Without his briefcase, he rushes to the back doors, claws them open, falls out of the bus, picks himself up, and runs down the street, ruining his pretty-boy hair in the rain. Like I pointed the gun at him intentionally or with malice aforethought or something.

Bag Lady shuffles real quiet to the back door and climbs out.

Now, there's no one left except me and Mr. Gun.

❀

The rain pounds on the roof, the wipers *swish swish creak swish,* and all the weight of my whole life drains out of my head, down my arms, through my hands, into the gun, and it feels like that's where everything that ever happened to me belongs. I put the gun behind my belt, and it feels good. Heavy, but a good kind of heavy.

I sit down in my seat and pull the lever to close the bus doors. When I light my cigarette, the flame of the match shakes, and that's when I notice my shirt is clinging to me. I drag a few deep ones into my lungs, and hold them as long as I can, till my heart slows down. I turn off the wipers, lean back in the seat, and pull down my paperback.

Raskolnikov's what I need right now, but I don't open the book yet. I shut off the bus. There's no sound but the rain. No sound but the rain and the pounding of my heart. Nothing but the rain and my heartbeat and the heavy solid weight of the gun digging into my body.

It feels good.

It feels real good.

Feels like what I've been looking for.

All my life.

Heart of a Lonely Hunter

*I*t's the guys in Group who say what I'm feeling is "primal loneliness" or some kinda crap like that. You say you don't know what to call it yet. I say I been kicked in the guts, and left in the Dumpster to die. Hurts more than the time the Marengo Brothers ambushed me in the alley behind Sol's place, and shoved so many calling cards between my ribs it looked like Doc Frankenstein got holda me. The guys in Group can call this pain whatever they want. All I know, for real, is that whatever this pain is, it can kill somebody else even if it don't kill you.

I had that pain my whole life. Long before I met Joanna. I never told you about Joanna? You sure? Well, she was one fine, phat lady, that Joanna. Smoother than smooth. Slicker than slick. Hotter than a two-pronged billy-goat. And when she smiled — man, oh, man — it was like every gang in the country give up its phat-est lady, rolled her into one, and give me the girl with everything I ever wished for. I was crazy to be with Joanna.

She liked me, too. She liked doing me. The other girls, they act like they was doing me a favor, or doing a job, or thinking of some other guy the whole time, but not Joanna. She wasn't faking it or nothing, and that's a natural fact. After what happened with them Marengo Brothers, I got myself better tuned in to people. In fact, I turned myself into a regular Geiger-counter like them scientists measure earthquakes with. Yeah, I got so I could tell real tremors from fake, and Joanna's was real. That's one of them things made me like her better than any of them other girls, I guess.

After she moved in with me, Joanna never forgot her place or tried bossing me around, like my Mom use to do to her guys, which is probably why half of them left. Joanna didn't sit around the house in her bathrobe all day watching soaps or game shows neither, like Mom done, which is probably why the other half of her guys split. No, Joanna worked hard every night, yet she cooked, done laundry and ironing, and kept the place picked up so I wasn't never embarrassed to bring any of my Boys to the place. And I never once had to pop her for smarting off or fooling around neither. Like I said, Joanna was for real.

❀

It wasn't too long after she moved in that I started in noticing the pain was gone. That ache that been twisting around in my guts as long as I could remember wasn't there no more. I mean, it was really gone, first time in my life. Next thing you know, I'm crazy-mad for Joanna, and I'm needing her, too, more than I need cigarettes or the pipe, more than I need Bobby to run for me, or Joey to drive me 'round the 'hood, proper-like.

Next thing, word on the Street — she done what the Marengo Brothers couldn't. Yo, what kinda shit is that? Couldn't have none of that bull-shit, know what I'm saying? Had to bust a couple jaws, take out a few meth-houses, show everybody I was still on top of my game, you know? I mean, I don't mind no jokes or slings between me and my Boys, but if people's dissing me or calling out my name, I gotta stand up, know what I mean? Hell, ain't no Zombie just 'cause I got myself a regular woman. Even Old Man Wexler's got hisself a girl, and he ain't nothing but rich.

When I told Joanna how much I liked her, she smiled and brushed her fingers along my jaw. Next thing, I start daydreaming about making it permanent with Joanna. Yeah, I know. Me, Johnny Bingo, with one of my own girls. Nobody north of 89th woulda believed it. Wouldn't have believed it myself if you'd ever told me. That ache in my gut was gone, though, and I tell you how serious it got, Man: I even started thinking there was more to life than the Streets. Can't believe it, can you? Neither could I.

The day I caught myself thinking about little Johnny Bingos running around, and smiling about it, was the day I decided to marry Joanna. I got her a ring — not hot or swapped or nothing — everything legit. From outta Old Man Wexler's jewelry store. Of course, outta the case in front. Nobody can say Johnny Bingo don't do it up right, even if Old Man Wexler hisself come outta his office to shake my hand and give me a nice discount deal.

Before I had a chance to ask Joanna, though, she done something that made that old pain smash me upside the head, harder than ever.

I left the pool hall earlier than usual 'cause I wanted to surprise my Woman. I bought some flowers off the corner Bag Lady, and put them in a glass on the kitchen table. Yeah, I always been kinda sentimental.

So, there I was, in the kitchen, flowers on the table, Champagne in the fridge, the ring in its Valentine's red-velvet box, when I hear a noise from the bedroom that makes my heart go like a Uzi. See, that's where I got my stash and my cash, in a floor-safe in the closet, so right away I'm reaching for my piece. Second, Joanna's usually sleeping that time of day. I chamber a round, and go down the hall, real slow.

I push the bedroom door with my foot, and what I saw, man, it made my heart stop. Joanna wasn't alone. And if that ain't bad enough, she ain't with no guy. I know you ain't gonna believe this, but she was with a tang. Yeah, you heard me right. One of my own girls, no less, one so new I ain't even done her myself yet. The new tail's eyes get like headlights when she sees me, like I'm Eddie the Goon or Big Tony Baloney from Brooklyn, and I ain't even aiming at her. She jump outta the bed so fast, she look like the Road Runner only she don't say *beep-beep*. Joanna, she don't move at all.

The new pootie grab her clothes, jabbering Puerto Rican or Mexican or some other Spic language, while Joanna lean over to the nightstand for a smoke. She lounge in the bed, smoking, looking at me, while the new pink-taco scrabble outta the place with only half her clothes on, shrieking Spic all the way down the hallway while Joanna keep on blowing smoke toward the ceiling.

That's when the pain come back, that pain I thought was gone forever. And stupid me. You know what I'm worrying about? That Champagne and them dumb flowers.

I'm thinking how it musta been a lie, every single bit of it, tremors and all, but I'm also thinking how that fine bottle of Champagne's probably getting warm and them flowers is wilting.

Yeah, love do make you stupid, don't it?

How could Joanna be with anybody after she been with Johnny Bingo? How could she ever be with a beave, especially some cha-cha? Maybe Johnny Bingo ain't no Denzel after what them Marengo Brothers done to my face and nose, but at least I'm a man, ain't I? That's what I'm standing there thinking, with that pain lynching my insides, while Joanna swing them fine legs of hers legs outta the bed and stand up, stretching like a cat just woke up from a nap in the sun.

She say something when she go by me. My Nine hanging down by my leg, my face turned toward this ho who just made all the pain of my whole life come back, and when I take holda her arm, she don't even feel like she's mine no more.

"Leggo," she say.

Just like that. To Johnny Bingo she say that: "Leggo."

All a sudden my legs is back working. I follow Joanna into the kitchen. She dump the flowers in the trash. She pour herself a glass of Scotch and open the fridge for some ice. She yank out the Champagne and the bottle break when she throw it in the sink. Joanna lean against the counter, smoking, drinking. After she drain the glass of Scotch, she pour herself another. When she shake her head, her dark hair fall around her face. That's when I realize she laughing. I ain't.

"I'm leaving," she say.

I reach out for her, so she remember she my Lady, but she put her hand against my chest and push.

"Don't make no fool outta yourself, Johnny."

Don't make no fool outta myself? Is them the words that just come outta her mouth? Don't make no fool outta myself?

Johnny Bingo ain't no fool.

Johnny Bingo ain't never been no fool in his whole life.

That's when something happens, something way down deep inside me, something hard and cold and blacker than the pain tangled up inside of me. It's worse than what them Marengo Brothers done to me 'cause, after all, I did hijack they truckload of DVD/Blu-Ray players and sell them without giving them no cut, so I kinda did deserve what I got from them. But Joanna and me, we belong to each other. She's my Woman. She can't just walk away without Johnny Bingo having no say-so. That ain't the way it goes. The pain's so bad, it's like... it's like...

✿

Nah, I still don't remember much of what happened after that. My hands holding onto something. Joanna looking surprised. Maybe she trying to say something. Noise in my head. Me telling Joanna how much I love her. She saying she sorry for what she done and she ain't gonna never do it no more. One of the po-lice-mans throwing up his dinner, and another one calling me "animal" and "crazy." I don't remember much else.

Prosecution say lot more done happened, though. Po-lice-mans, they show me pictures of what they say I done to Joanna before they got there. But I keeps telling them and telling them that Johnny Bingo never done nothing like that to his Main Squeeze. He don't even own no hunting knife. Why'd he do something like that to his very Own One-and-Only when he love her so much?

✿

I stretch out on my bunk, trying to remember, in my own brain, not in some po-lice-man's pictures. Makes my head hurt. I talk about it with you, and sometimes with the guys in Group. They don't listen good as you. They throw words at me like sucker-punches — "denial," "loneliness," "abandonment," "sexually abusive childhood," and "confused sexual orientation."

I stay on the ropes just like Ali: Ropa-Dope, only Johnny Bingo ain't no dope. When the guys in Group get tired, I punch the shit outta them words. Don't need no fancy new words for what I'm feeling. Already got the only word I need. Pain.

Capital P-A-I-N.

Guard Bill's the only one who ever calls it straight. He never asks no stupid questions neither. That's 'cause he had a girl like Joanna once. 'Course, his story didn't turn out like mine. He still understands, though. Guard Bill passes me one of his cigarettes and we both stand there, smoking, not talking, and it's almost like the bars between us ain't even there. Guard Bill's the only one here besides me who knows what I'm talking about.

'Course, I know you trying, Doc, but I guess you gotta go through it yourself to really be in the situation, you know?

Been going on 13 years now, but that pain hurts more than ever. Sometimes it makes me think of jumping Guard Bill out in the yard so one of the Tower Bulls can end it for me, but I wouldn't do that to Guard Bill. These prison Bulls, they's amateurs. They ain't as good with guns as most of us are, and I wouldn't want Guard Bill to get shot after he been so good to me. No, Johnny Bingo ain't that kinda guy.

Sometimes I think of stripping the bunk, ripping up the sheets, knotting them into a rope around my throat, and hanging myself from the hot water pipes, but...

No, you got it all wrong. It ain't 'cause Johnny Bingo's afraid of dying. I seen dying every day of my life. I seen dying so close up I know what his damn breath smell like, so don't be telling Johnny Bingo he's afraid. Johnny Bingo ain't afraida nothing. Don't you be calling out my name, or we be having us a talk in the yard when nobody ain't looking.

It's just, I don't know how it's gonna be on the other side, is all. It might be cold and dark. Or it could be like Mom's old man Jake always said it was — fire and sulphur. I don't know if Joanna's gonna be waiting for me over there. I'd like to be with her if she was there, but she might look like them po-lice photos, and if she look like that... well, yeah, sometimes women do take a helluva long time to forgive.

Every night, after my cigarette with Guard Bill, I stretch out on my cot, listen to the other guards as they go past the cells, listen to the sound of they clubs against the bars when they tell us to get some sleep, to the sound of someone's lighter in the dark, to the sound of my blood as it pounds through my ears.

Mostly what I listen to is the pain, and it's a cold, dark, ugly sound, 'specially when nobody but you can hear it the same way. In the dark, with nothing but the pain, I get spooked. Maybe that pain'll finish what them Marengo Brothers started.

So far, though, nothing.

So I wait.

For another cigarette with Guard Bill. For another session with you, or Group with Doc Thompson and the guys. For a ruling on one of my appeals.

For the hangman.

Song of New Jersey

If I know a song of Africa...
does Africa know a song of me?

Isak Dinesen

S weet land of liberty" — and all that other crap — "of thee I sing." Plenty of people singing in the 'hood these days, but not about liberty. They not singing with they mouths. They singing how to stay alive. Only thing there is, know what I'm saying?

"Pilgrims' pride?" Man, what you talking about? Pilgrims, they ain't got no pride. I mean, if you a pilgrim in this 'hood, you die, ain't no way around it. Look around you, Bro. Only a pilgrim gonna walk around here without his Boys. If you ain't got no Boys, at the very minimest, you gotta have you a piece. Boys, they better than a Nine. See, a Brother's got his Boys, he don't have to watch his own back all the time. His Boys do it for him. That's they job. A Brother's got his Boys, nobody be dissing him or calling out his name or trying to take his turf, you know?

A Brother's got his Boys, he can concentrate hisself on the three most important things in the world — babes, bucks, and stash, yeah. Without stash, you ain't got no bucks; without bucks, no babes. Only pilgrims don't got they priorities straight, so how can they have pride? The answer is — they cain't, and they don't. That's all I got to say about pilgrims 'cause they pilgrims.

"Land where my fathers died" — now I cain't be talking about no fathers 'cause I don't even know who the dude was, but plenty of the HomeBoys be dying; plenty be dying every single day.

Sometimes it's 'cause they playing like pilgrims, going 'round without they Nines or they Boys. Sometimes, it's just the way things go down: ain't no way to stop it.

Nobody said this shit was easy, but it don't have to be no war. They's something called negotiation — what some of the brothers ain't learned yet. That's why they still pilgrims. That's why they still dying, see?

❀

Some of the brothers, they think negotiation is what they done to BlackJack Freddy — pulling up in front of his place on 89th emptying the Uzi's, and squealing away before The Man gets there. Hell, that ain't no kinda negotiation.

Besides, they didn't just get BlackJack Freddy. They got BlackJack Freddy's girl and her little boy — that's cold, man, that's downright *Bru-tal-i-tee*, capital *B*.

Brother's got business with another Brother, he do it man-to-man, conversating face-to-face. If that don't work, he sends his Boys with a message, not straight away with no Uzi's. If none of that don't work, a Brother's gotta re-evaluate the situation, look over the other Brother's weak spots, calculate the best way to gain the upper hand in the situation, and then re-negotiate.

Maybe he do that by hijacking stash — that always make a other party willing to sit down and smoke with you. He ain't got no stash coming in for you to hijack, you pick one of his Boys — one — no more than one — you pick one of his Boys to make a example of.

Like what Mister Winston done to Johnny Bingo's Boy Bobby.

❀

See, Bobby's fingers got a little too sticky, like that white powder's made from Elmer's and Bobby couldn't help hisself. Yeah, everybody's fingers, they get a little sticky from time to time — I ain't saying we all saints, but Bobby's fingers — they got so white he coulda passed. Everybody in the 'hood knows it was Johnny Bingo hisself told Bobby to get his sticky little fingers in there, but Mister Winston, see, he knows how to negotiate.

He takes care of Bobby's sticky fingers, Mr. Winston does, but in a way that Johnny Bingo gets the message loud and clear, and right away gives Mister Winston the 77th turf back, which Mister Winston and his Boys have been negotiating for. Johnny Bingo is sorry, Bobby ain't got no fingers to be sticky with no more, and Mister Winston is happy.

That's what negotiations is for — to cut down any trouble the Boys get theyselves in to. 'Course, if the first step of negotiation don't work, if making a example of a Brother's Boy don't work, then you proceed to the next step — the Brother hisself.

Like The Breed done to Jimmy James a couple of years back.

❀

See, The Breed, he had this babe, Vanessa was her name, and she was one high class babe. I ain't never met her personal myself, but I heard from Keefer whose twin Keef saw her at the mall jewelry store that she was one helluva babe. 'Course, what else kinda babe is The Breed gonna have?

This Vanessa, who belong to The Breed, which everybody and his Brothers and his Boys and they cousins know, this Vanessa, she disappears one weekend. *Poof.* Just like a magician show. Nobody seen her go and nobody know where she is. The Breed, he frantic by Saturday night.

Then one of Jimmy James' Boys who wanna move up to being one of The Breed's Boys, he lets it slip how if The Breed was to go over to this certain Sunset Inn on the north side of the 'hood, The Breed might find something of so much value that he might like to reward this ambitious Boy of Jimmy James by making him into a Boy of The Breed.

The Breed, he go there, with just about all of his Boys on accounta he don't know exactly what he gonna find there, even though all his Boys gotta pretty good idea what's there. The Breed and his Boys gets there, find Jimmy James hisself in a certain non-negotiable position with Vanessa, and next thing you know, word is out that pieces of Jimmy James his own self is scattered all over the 'hood, as a warning, so to speak, and Jimmy James' ambitious Boy is one of The Breed's very own — driving The Breed hisself around town, no less —and everybody's happy again.

Vanessa, she ain't so happy no more now she's back working the Streets, but that scar, when she lean against some car, it ain't that bad, and sometimes her hair sorta cover it. Me, myself, I think it's kinda interesting, but then I always did like the bad girls.

So, you see how The Breed negotiated with Jimmy James — not sending his Boys over to kill innocent little kids and they Baby-Mamas with Uzis. See, when everybody does the art of negotiation proper, then things go the way they suppose to.

Then us Boys can have a little free time, do a little singing, so to speak, check out the Babes, strut our stuff a little bit. It's sweet, you know what I mean? We talking about pride so big you can feel it, pride so big you can hear it ringing all over the 'hood.

"Sweet land of liberty, let freedom ring."

Now that kind pride, that kinda sweet — I can tell you all about that.

Working the Room

*T*ake a bath."

"You're the first one tonight; I'm clean."

"I want to watch. I want to stand behind the door and watch."

I sigh as I undress. At least he's better than the guy who wanted me to play dead.

❀

"Play dead?" I said. "How am I suppose to do that?"

He looked real surprised, like most everybody in the world knew the answer except me.

He sighed real loud and said, "You don't move, you close your eyes, you don't say nothing."

When I was laying on the bed thinking I was doing a pretty good "dead," he got a little rough and I made a noise, not on purpose, and he hit me, shouting how I ruined it, and that it was all my fault he lost it.

Play Dead, my ass.

❀

Now here I am with this cute guy who could get all the girls he wanted if you ask me, and he wants me to take a bath while he hides behind the door and watches. Whatever. It don't cost extra. I do the bath, real careful not to mess my makeup and hair. Usually it's the fat, bald, ugly businessmen who hide behind curtains and doors to watch, but I guess everybody's got his own head-game.

"Now go lie on the bed," he says as I'm drying off.

I lay on the bed, posing myself like I did for "Dead Guy," only with my eyes open. I'm on the bed, waiting and waiting and waiting. Finally, I get off the bed and go back to the bathroom. He's looking at pictures, and touching himself.

"If you got pictures, why do you need me?"

"Get back on the bed," he says, and he follows me out. "Can I tie you up?"

"That's extra."

"I can afford it."

He opens his duffel bag and takes out black nylon stockings. Not pantyhose that have been cut up. Stockings. After he ties me up, he holds up a folded handkerchief and one more stocking.

"Open your mouth," he says.

"That's gonna mess up my lipstick," I say.

"I can afford it,"

"Maybe I don't wanna do my whole makeup over. You ever think of that?"

"Did you ever think I'd give you a big tip?"

"How big? 'Cause you're really taking a long time."

"Three times what you charge."

"You're gonna pay me *and* give me three times that as the tip?"

"Jesus, you're a greedy little whore," he says.

I'm already real tired of this pretty little rich boy. Since he picked me up at the diner before I had a chance to eat anything, I just want him to get it over with so I can go get myself some food.

"I'll pay you, and give you the three times as the tip."

"Okay. You can do the gag."

"Good. 'Cause it don't work for me if you don't scream," he says.

"I don't need no gag to scream good."

"I need it."

When he's tying the gag, I'm thinking he's like the "Play-Dead" guy and I start to think about all them bills in his wallet, and how all them bills are gonna look real good in my bag. I could start my own little savings account and think of really heading for the West Coast to see what kinda work I could get on a soap opera. I got my looks, I've worked real hard to keep my figure, all my clients say I got talent. The thing I ain't got is money — that's gonna change tonight. I'm getting more than a tip from this boy, wasting my whole night. His type always takes a really long bath afterward. I'm gonna take everything he's got: ID, cash, debit cards, credit cards, and iPhone, too.

He goes over to the duffel bag, takes something out, and crawls up onto the bed. When he kneels over me, I start twisting and screaming.

"Not yet," he says, and he holds up the knife.

⊛

So, he's not like Dead Guy at all. He's like the guy from Cleveland who brought his kid's toy gun and wanted me to make like he was robbing me or kidnapping me or something. He held his kid's toy gun to my head while he was doing it. He came so hard and fast, he got it all over my dress, so I made him buy me a new one, buy me dinner, and give me a tip besides.

Toy gun...

Rubber knives...

⊛

I'm kinda disappointed. This one's so good-looking and strong and all, I thought he'd do better than the Toy-gun guy. You can't have everything. He's kneeling and I'm thinking how I can go out to the West Coast when he pushes the tip of the knife against my breast.

It hurts, but only a little, just so I can't tell if it's rubber or plastic, and I start the screaming routine, real careful not to twist too much on accounta not wanting to get my hair and makeup all messed up. He's undoing his jeans 'cause he's really ready, so I go into my moaning and petrified routine when he presses the knife harder against my breast. Hey, it don't even feel like plastic. I try to jerk my knee so he knows it really hurts. He leans down real close, all the time pressing down on the knife.

"Don't move, bitch. You don't do nothing I don't tell you to do,"

Jesus, there's blood. That's it for this girl. He ain't got enough money for this. I got my Hollywood TV career to think of. When I bump him with my hips to get him off me, he smiles, but real scary. I start trying to get my wrists out of the stockings tied to the bedframe.

"You got real nice ones," he says, moving the knife real light all over my breasts. "Too bad they gotta go."

Oh, Jesus... oh, please, don't... oh, God, please... I won't steal your money... You can have this one for free, that's what a good sport I am, only don't... oh, God, no, please don't... He's moving so hard on me... and the knife... it's burning... I think I'm going to be sick... oh, please, please...

God, if You get me out of this one, I'll never do it again.

I'll go straight... I'll go get my kids outta foster care and be a good mom to them...

I'll get a real job... even if it's only minimum wage, even if I have to be a waitress again... oh, please, please...

I promise...

Fame

Don't move," he says. "You'll spoil it."
The bed groans under his weight. My wrists and ankles strain at the ropes. He shows me the knife again.
"You're number seventeen."
I jerk, choking on the gag.
"You'll be famous," he says. "Just like you wanted."
The blade comes down.
"Say *thank you*," he says.

Part Three

On n'est jamais si hereux ni si
malhereux qu'on s'imagine.

(One is never as happy or
unhappy as one imagines.)

Duc de la Rochefoucauld
Maximes 49

Rebellion in the Promised Land

rankly, he's beginning to frighten us. We had to make a decision among ourselves. He's changed, and we don't like it. Hadn't we just escaped from a land where one man decided the condition and fate of all our lives?

One day, for no reason that he revealed to us, he decided the men should no longer wear jewelry, not even rings or necklaces. Next day, he announced the women should refrain from wearing rings, bracelets, earrings, nose-rings, everything. There were rumors — he was going to take all the money and jewelry himself, to safeguard it. My wife and I weren't the only ones who sewed our few valuables into the linings of our clothes. We're still loyal to him, but we have an obligation to protect our families, don't we?

Early one morning, a great cry circulated in the camp — he'd called a meeting. We hurried to his tent without even finishing our breakfasts. We thought someone had died, our pack animals had contracted some contagious disease, or the native population had become offended by our passage through their homeland and were about to declare war on us. Trembling and cold, we huddled around his tent in the faint pre-dawn light, afraid to breathe.

His announcement was worse than we'd anticipated. It wasn't war or disease or death. He'd decided to ration the food. During the night, some of his family had gone through the camp, appropriating the food and taking it to his tent to ensure we had sufficient supplies to reach our destination. My wife gripped my arm so tightly it hurt. Food was all around us, every morning, on every bush and tree, *manna* from the Lord Himself, Blessèd Be His Name. In every waterhole, enough water for us and all our animals. Rationing? Had he gone mad spending so much time up in the mountains?

My brother eased his way through the crowd to stand beside me.

"Benjamin," he said in a whisper, "what should we do?"

Better not to talk there. Who were completely loyal to him? Who were frightened, like us? Early the next morning, seven of us went out to gather surplus food — as a security measure — only to discover that every branch, every vine, every twig had been picked clean.

That was when we began to use signals and signs, to sound out others, to meet secretly at the furthest edges of the camp. We were more than frightened of him. We were certain we would all die in the desert.

⚘

Then he went back into the mountains. His wife said he'd had a vision and had retreated to contemplate how best to lead us, and though it sounded like the very type of thing he'd do, we insisted that his wife show us the stores of food, money, and jewels.

After we saw the supplies, we relaxed a little. Since he hadn't taken them with him, perhaps he was merely meditating, seeking guidance, praying to The Holy One Above. It was good those weeks he was in the mountains — better than when he was here with us. For one thing, everyone was less circumspect. People laughed more, argued less, became friendlier and more affectionate.

My Rebecca convinced his wife to release some of the women's jewelry, to wear to David's and Mary's wedding banquet, and they forgot to return it to her safekeeping after the party, so the women were happier — they looked prettier, too, and they harped at their men less. Samuel's sister was his wife's cousin, so she persuaded his wife to distribute some of the wine to celebrate the birth of Samuel's first grandson, as was only right and proper.

Everyone in the camp was more jovial, relaxed, and extremely grateful to her for being so gracious and understanding. We extended her much genuine affection. His own brother Aaron convinced her that the morale of the camp would improve if we had a celebration. By then, she didn't need much persuasion. She was happier with her own husband in the mountains, too.

Everyone was excited about the celebration. We dressed in our finest clothes, drank, danced, ate, and drank more. Because it had been so long since any of us had had wine, most of us got drunk. In fact, I was so unused to the wine that I fell asleep quite early, while everyone else was still dancing.

Waking the next morning, I found the camp in chaos. He'd returned in the midst of the revelry. While in the mountains, he'd written something on two stone tablets, something he claimed came from the Lord our God Himself, and he'd come down in the night to share it with us. When he saw what was happening in the camp, he raised the tablets and, with a mighty roar, smashed them against the mountainsides.

He tore through the camp like an Egyptian, his fists flailing, feet kicking, screams cowering the bravest. He toppled the golden calf into the great fire, ignoring the shrieks of those who tried to save the melting gold by dragging it out, slashing at them with his staff. I found my wife huddled in the corner of some rocks, against our collapsed tent, weeping into the sleeves of her silk dress.

By the time my brother came to me, there were at least forty men with us, including his own brother Aaron. My brother Eli looked at Aaron, who nodded, and I knew it was time.

Now we wait.

It must be when he's alone.

It must be in the dark.

We would never have chosen violence. He's forced it on us. He's the only one who must be taken care of. We won't even warn his wife beforehand. Afterward, we'll take his body into the mountains. He can be with his God. Aaron will assume power quickly and efficiently. No questions will be asked aloud. We'll continue our journey to our homeland, the land The Holy One Above promised us as our birthright.

So, it's decided. We shake hands. Before we disperse, my brother steps up to Aaron.

"What about the tablets, the ones he brought down from the mountains?"

"What about them?"

"Should we try to piece them together and read them?"

Aaron frowns as he rubs his chin with his hands.

"What if they really came from... the Lord?" says my brother Eli.

Aaron straightens up, and for the first time, I realize how much taller he is than his brother.

"We'll crush the broken tablets without reading them," says Aaron. "We'll leave them with Moses' body."

Though we glance at each other, we say nothing.

From that moment on, all of us understand everything that must be done.

Madonna, with Child

Ｎone of them is listening to me. She is a good girl. I knew that the first time I saw her. She was getting lamb from the butcher and as he wrapped the meat in the linen, I looked at her. Yes, I stared at her. She's so beautiful. I'd never seen anyone so pale and delicate. She blushed when she saw me staring, and when she bent her head, some of her hair slipped out from under her veil, and I longed to touch that raven-colored hair. After the butcher handed her the meat, she left, and I went to the doorway of the shop to watch her walk down the road.

She looked back once — at me.

That's when I knew I wanted her.

"You didn't have her, did you?" says Caleb.

"Please tell us you haven't been with her," says Jonah.

"We all know how attached to her you are," says Luke.

"I love her," I say.

"Yes, well, if you want to call it love, we won't quibble..."

"All we're saying is, don't ruin your life by marrying the girl."

"No one will blame you."

"Everyone knows her reputation."

"Everyone except you, apparently," says Jonah.

When I drop my tools to I swing at him, he ducks.

I think of that first night she came to me. We couldn't be together at my house, because of my daughters from my deceased wife — may the Lord God be with her — and we couldn't be at her house because of her parents, so we met in the foothills of the Highlands, surrounded by wildflowers. At first she wouldn't even sit close enough for me to touch her hand, she was so scared and shy.

Not that I would've touched her. I respected her. I was already half in love with her. We sat together for the longest time. We didn't talk. We sat there, in the shadows, in silence, hardly looking at each other, and then I walked her home.

⚜

"Women like her are always the cleverest," says Jonah.
"She's a nice girl."
"We know someone," says Luke.
"He'll say he's been with her."
"He'll claim the child is his."
"And his price is very reasonable."
"He's done it before," says Caleb, "so we know he's reliable."
"He's a man of his word..."
"Am I not a man of my word?" I say.

⚜

I don't remember how many times we met before she let me hold her hand. Her skin was so soft. I was ashamed to touch it, what with my hand so rough and callused from the shop and my work. I wanted to kneel before her and kiss her fingers, the back of her hand, her palm, but I thought of my daughters and how they needed a mother. I thought of how much I wanted a son — many sons — to take the place of the ones who'd died almost as soon as they were born. So I did nothing but hold her fair, soft hand in mine.

⚜

"I've already said I'd marry her."
"But you haven't been with her, have you?" says Caleb.
"I shook hands with her father. I ate her mother's lentil and onion stew; I drank wine with the two of them."
"Oh, by the Name of the Holy One Above," says Luke, "don't tell us you've been with her."
"Please, don't even say *once*," says Jonah.
"If he has, then she planned this perfectly," says Luke.
"You didn't tell anyone else that you'd marry her, did you?"
"I didn't tell the whole town, if that's what you mean."
"You didn't tell your daughters, did you?"
"They met her. They liked each other."

"Everyone likes her."
"That's what we're trying to tell you."
"Only you're not listening."
"I brought wine to her parents…"
"There's still a chance we can save you."
"From what?"
"From her."

❀

I'd promised to marry her before I ever kissed her, before I held her in my arms, before I touched her neck where her hair curled gently away from it. I made that promise many, many times. I made it because I was in love with her. Because I am in love with her. What kind of man would I be if I broke that promise?

❀

"Tell us. We have to know so we can help you..."
"She says the baby's mine."
"So, you have been with her?"
"Once."
"That's all she needed."
"We can still use that man..."
"I think so, too. We should hire him..."
"Am I a man who abandons an innocent girl and her baby?"
"If the baby's not yours..."
"How do I know it's not mine?"
"We've been trying to tell you."
"Haven't you been listening?"
Suddenly, my hands want to grab something and crush it, my heels want to grind something into the dust, my mouth wants to taste blood. The three of them scatter to the far side of the shop. Luke picks up an unfinished table leg and holds it like a club in front of him. Jonah cowers behind a chair while Caleb hides behind a refinished door. One by one, they apologize, they promise never to mention it again, they promise to stand up with me at my wedding.

After they leave, I try to work, but I almost cut off my thumb I'm so distressed. I put the tools away. I make dinner for the girls, and afterward, while they're cleaning up, I go for a walk.

59

I don't mean to go to her house, I don't mean to go anywhere at all, but there I am, outside her window, calling her by making the sound of a dove. I pace in the orchard until she gets there. We walk to the foothills. Once there, she tries to kiss me. I hold her away.

"I have to ask you something."

She sits down on one of the fallen trees and looks up at me.

"No matter what the answer is, I'll marry you. I've made that promise, and I won't break it, no matter what anyone says about you."

She frowns just a bit, the frown making a line between her eyes.

The moonlight makes her look even paler than usual. Her hands are in her lap. She sighs deeply before she looks me bravely in the face, and I know they must be wrong about her. They must be. I clear my throat several times before the Lord God Above — Holy Be His Name — gives me the courage to speak.

"I'll only ask this once. We'll never speak of it again. For the rest of our lives together."

She nods.

"Mary," I say, "is the child mine?"

"Oh, Joseph," she says, looking up at me with so much love in her eyes, speaking in a voice as soft as an angel's, "I do hope so."

The Gardens in Her Eyes

She has enough power over him already, so I'd never tell her that he's ready to give up his teaching for her. Why, she's turned him in to a mass of unbaked bread dough. What else could you expect when a man like him meets a woman like her? If he's not as green as an unripe fig or as stone-hard as a pomegranate plucked before its time, I don't know who is.

Bitter? Why shouldn't I be? She was mine before she discovered he was going to be running things. Therefore, chronologically, ethically, morally, she belongs to me. He claims I'm his best friend, yet he didn't honor our friendship by resisting any feelings she aroused in him.

I don't care how fine the gauze dress she was wearing, how exotic the oil behind her ears, how soft her breasts when they pressed against his neck as she leaned over him at the table. He should've remembered his love and loyalty for me. For me. He's the one who should've turned away from her. There are plenty of other women who'd abandon everything for him: husband, children, home. They're just as beautiful as she is, just as wealthy. Why did he have to take my woman?

Oh, dear Lord in Heaven, why can't You help me forget her? Help me find another? Every night, lying lonely and alone on my bedroll on the sleeping platform opposite them, listening to the sounds of their lovemaking, aching for her, I pray You will send me someone new to love.

At the same time, though, I'm thinking of how to hurt both of them, the way they hurt me.

❁

She thinks he's going to be the leader; she believes him so loyal and committed, honest and devout. He's nothing but my wooden toy. Tomorrow, to prepare himself for his work, he's going away,

61

after he's baptized, into the Wilderness, for almost two months, and he's not telling anyone. Not even her. I'm the only one who'll know where he is. When he comes back, he'll be ready. Because this time, I've finally fashioned a vision of himself that fits him. He's already tried it on. He likes it. He's going to the Wilderness.

While he's there — the thirst, hunger, heat, visions — metamorphosis. When he returns, he'll lead other men, he'll make sacrifices, he'll fight the corruption in the Promised Land even if only in a symbolic fashion. He'll be the man we've all been waiting for.

And he won't have time for her.

She'll be stunned. She'll stare at him, her red lips parted in that pouty way she has. Her violet-lined eyelids will flutter a little, as if she's trying to see him through smoke. Some part of her body will brush against his — breasts, hip, thigh. It's not for nothing she wears those gauzy gowns, lets the material slip down off her shoulders, stands between him and the light to remind him what he's missing. Oh, yes, she's good, very good. But this time, it won't work. This time, I've invented a version of himself that's greater than her charms.

This time he's seen a vision of himself glorious enough to be worth the fight, magnificent enough to be worth the sacrifice, blessèd enough to be worth death itself. He's had the vision from God himself — not from an angel, mind you, but from the Lord God himself.

Coincidentally, of course, God happened to deliver this supreme vision to him after a night of heavy meat and spiced wine provided by yours truly, and, not coincidentally, God's vision of him happens to correspond exactly with the vision of him that I've painstakingly constructed over the last few years.

Ah, yes, God does move in mysterious ways.

❀

Why use him instead of leading the people myself? For practical reasons — he's taller, younger, and, I admit, better looking. Besides, he's gotten himself quite a reputation as a teacher and a healer in the past few years. That, combined with his charm and good looks make him an ideal leader, albeit a figurehead.

Men and women alike clamor to follow him. Men and women alike fall in love with him, though for different reasons. Men and women alike will sacrifice themselves on any altar I construct for him.

When he comes back from the Wilderness, he'll believe in himself so completely, he'll be able to work miracles. Others will believe in him so totally that they'll raise him above them. They'll call him God's messenger. They'll say he's Adam born again to take us back to the Garden.

No, they'll say he's God's own belovèd son.

And they'll believe he's God's Chosen One because I say that he is.

❦

After she's slept alone long enough, she'll realize that he has, indeed, changed, and that he doesn't belong to her anymore. That he belongs to me. That she belongs to me. If I say so. I'll be the only man she'll ever be with again. Every time she turns around, it'll be my face she sees; when she listens, it'll be my voice she hears; when she aches in the night, it'll be my body she longs for.

All she has to do is reach out her braceleted arm, whisper my name in that throaty voice of hers, stand near enough for me to smell the musk of her perfume — and I'll remind her what it's like to be taken by a real man.

What it's like to pant and sweat under a man's weight, what it's like to jam silk scarves into her mouth to muffle her cries when she's taken from behind, what's it's like to scratch and writhe and cry out her satisfaction.

She'll never be the same.

She'll never go back to him.

This time, I'm closing my hand around her. This time, every painted, perfumed inch of her belongs to me. Forever.

This time, when she opens herself in the night, it'll be my name she sighs, my mouth she kisses, my breath she tastes when she arches her back and moans her only lover's name, "Judas, oh, my dear, sweet Judas."

Golgotha, Mon Amour

Those eyes of his snared me like a fish, dragging me out of my life and into his. Now, when I look at all the parasites clinging to him, I see only a few dozen who've been touched as I was. It's in their eyes — anyone can see it. The rest of them are dragging the net down. They should all be thrown back into the sea. They haven't really been changed.

I'm not saying I was perfect before I met him. No, I'd never say that, though I'd already become the sort of person who could understand, who could see his vision, who could truly hear what he was saying. It was after I'd changed, after I'd found him, that I fell in love with him.

"You're jealous of them," he says, "because they love me, too."

I've wiped my feet on their betters. They leave bread crumbs and emptied wine flagons and broken crockery all over the floor. Vagrants, thieves, whores — they don't listen to a word he's saying. They want bread, wine, the clothes off his back, the shoes off his feet. After they've taken all they can, they'll grind him between their blackened teeth and spit him out in the dirt. I spent my life with people like that.

"And look how well you've turned out," he says, and he chucks me under the chin like I'm some orphan or stray dog that straggled home after him.

"I was already a changed woman by the time I met you. My husband changed me."

"I know," he says.

How could he know how much I'd changed? I'd given up spiced wine, baked meat, fried bread; I'd stopped painting my lips and my eyelids; I'd changed my gowns of gauze and silk for simple dresses of wool. Those were all frivolous, external changes. When I met him, it was my very heart that changed.

My blood ran hot then cold, my heart hammered then faltered, my skin was sweaty then clammy — and all that before he'd said a single word. All he'd done was look at me.

❀

"They're just... stealing from you," I say as he crawls into bed.

"Without them, I have no work," he says.

"There are plenty of people who need you and who can contribute to your ministry."

"I don't need their money. I don't want it," he says, starting to snore. "A man cannot serve... two... masters."

"Earning enough money... wake up... earning money to put bread on the table or lamb in the stewpot isn't serving two masters," I say, and he smiles at me in that way he has.

"I love you, more than any of the others," he says in that honeyed voice of his, and I'd feed those parasites and sycophants off my own plate to please him.

That's the power he has over me. He's taught me that love isn't just words. Only I've gotten nothing but words for months. Before he falls asleep, he kisses me on the cheek or on the forehead, like a brother kisses his sister. Why does he push my hand away when I try to show him my love? Why does he turn his head when I kiss him on the mouth? What kind of love is it that he has for me now? The same kind of love that he has for all those filth that he's saved?

❀

"The only kind of love he knows is his work," says his best friend, the bookkeeper. "His work will change the world."

I suspect the bookkeeper is pilfering.

If I could catch him, if I could see him slip one coin into his own pocket, I'd drag him by his curly red beard and dash him into the dirt, saying, "Look, this is the love he and the others have for you — thieves' love."

"I love him far more than you do," says the bookkeeper, "and I don't have to sleep with him to prove it. The proof of my love for him is in my respect for his work, my encouragement, my admiration."

I wanted to gouge his eyes out, that filthy little bookkeeper.

His work and the little money he does earn aren't the only things the bookkeeper admires: I've noticed the way the bookkeeper looks at me when we're alone, and it's not my face he's admiring.

❁

I'm not imagining it. Tonight, when I was putting the lentil stew, the onions, the bread, and the salt on the dining rug, he pressed his upper arm against me, against my breast.

That wasn't the first time, but it was the first time I've been sure that it wasn't an accident. He's done it several times. He pretends to be reaching for the stew or the bread — it doesn't matter which — it's the way he looks at me when he does it. He presses against me then bites that thick, full bottom lip of his with those straight teeth, letting it go slowly, never looking away from me. That bookkeeper — he's more than a thief and a liar — he'd betray him, his own best friend, if he could.

It isn't jealousy I feel as I hurry over to my place, my heart hammering, my cheeks flushed, my palms tingling.

"Please don't leave me alone tonight," I say in his ear, but he merely pats my leg and smiles at something the bookkeeper says.

Maybe he doesn't love me after all. Maybe his work is his only love, his only passion.

I get up from the dining rug fast, so he won't see the tears. I don't want him to stay out of pity. I don't want the bookkeeper to see my humiliation. I go to the other side of the room, my back toward them, and start scouring the pot with sand.

"If this is how he treats the woman he loves," I think, but my tears blur the pot I'm cleaning.

❁

"We're going to drink our wine in the courtyard," he says to me after they've eaten, and they're all rising from the dining rug, stretching, and picking up their wine-cups. "We'll take the olives and the bread with us."

I nod as all of them leave the main room. I put away the food, and clean the platters. As I'm placing the crocks and dishes away on the shelves, I hear a noise behind me.

"We're out of bread," says the bookkeeper.

He doesn't even use my name. He doesn't say "please." Like I'm a slave bought from a Roman auction block. I gather some warmed flat bread from the covered basket near the oven and take it over to where he stands. As I lay the bread on the serving platter, which isn't empty, he drops the platter of flatbread on the packed dirt floor, yanks me against him, his arms tight around my waist and back, his chest and hips hard against me.

His mouth is open on mine, his tongue forcing itself in. Before I can stop him, he's pressing his knee and thigh upward between my legs. I can't breathe, my fists are pounding his chest and shoulders, my nails are digging any bare skin I can reach, but something in my body is saying, "Yes, yes, this is how a man should be."

Suddenly, we hear a noise, and when the bookkeeper pushes me away from him — both of us panting like animals — we see him standing there in the doorway.

"Magdalena, Judas," he says, "what are you doing?"

In the Path of the Juggernaut

Juggernaut:
A belief to which people
sacrifice themselves or others.

"When, in all the years I've been stationed in this hideous desert province, when have you known me to actually hear one of these cases?"

"Yes, I know, my Lord, but the local dignitaries are in quite an uproar..."

"What local dignitaries?"

"The Priests, of course."

"I buy the Priests, you idiot. They can't be in an uproar against me."

I indicate to my slave the three bags I'm taking back home with me. To another, I point out the wrapped package on the bed. A gift for my wife. Silk scarves with elaborate embroidery and beading. From some far-off land by way of the Parthians, the vendor told me. My wife will be pleased.

"The Priests did get into an uproar about those Standards. Got nearly half the city's population into an uproar about it..."

"Do you want to be whipped?" I say.

"I'm... I'm your aide, sir."

"Do you think that means I can't have you whipped?"

"I'm not a slave, my Lord. I'm a citizen."

"Weren't you a slave at one time?" I say, rubbing my chin slowly and narrowing my eyes.

"Your lordship gave me my freedom."

"How long ago?"

"Ten years, sir."

"Very well, then, I suppose I won't have you whipped."

"Gratitude, my Lord."

One of the slaves ties my sandals while another adjusts my traveling cloak. As I glance around the room to see if I've forgotten anything, I hold out my wrists and hands so that the female slaves may put my bracelets and rings in place. When they're finished, they bow before slowly walking backward from my bedroom. The large Carthaginian who adjusted my cloak picks up my golden necklace which holds my great seal of office, lifts it over my head, puts it around my neck, and settles it against my chest. He's the only one tall enough to do it so that I don't have to bend my head. I give him his daily coin. As always, he closes his eyes as he slightly bows his head and leaves the room.

"The Priests are quite insistent that you hear these charges..."

"Which means the charges demand the death penalty?"

"Yes, sir."

"And the only death penalty the Priests can issue is 'death by stoning' for religious and moral issues such as blasphemy and adultery."

"Yes, sir."

"That means this is a case dealing with insurrection or rebellion against the Roman Empire?"

"It concerns a disturbance at the Temple... They say he disrupted the entire monetary system and made threats."

"Against Rome?"

"I'm not quite sure, my Lord."

"Why aren't you quite sure, Lucius?"

"He's one of the silent ones."

"One of the suicides, you mean."

"Yes, sir."

"I don't see any reason to stay in the city for that," I say. "I have to get back to Caesarea Maritima and the Mediterranean. You know I simply can't breathe here."

"The Priests know you haven't left the city yet..."

"Guilty as charged. Crucify him."

"They say he's scheming to set himself up as the new head of state..."

I laugh aloud.

"...that he commands thousands, tens of thousands — all willing to martyr themselves to his fanatical cause. They say if you don't destroy him now, chaos and rebellion..."

"Who is 'they'?"

"The Priests. Caiphas, most particularly."

"Where is he?"

"Caiphas or the prisoner?"

"I'm going to exile you to Germania when this is all over, Lucius."

"They're downstairs, my Lord. Both of them. All the others are with them."

❁

All the Priests bow, as do the guards, when I sweep into the Great Hall. Immediately I notice that despite their reputed terror of the man, he's not bound in any way. He's no Rebel, at least not the kind they're accusing him of being. All the Priests want to speak. And they don't even shut up despite the fact that there's no translator present.

I send for one of the guards who speaks *koinē,* the common Greek language left by Alexander's soldiers that the soldiers and the shopkeepers still use to communicate. None of the Priests speak it. One of the shopkeepers does, though, and he begs my permission to come forward and translate with the guard.

At once the Priests start babbling that the prisoner is a healer, a magician, an exorcist, while some of the others present insist he's only a teacher, until finally the two translators can't keep up, and they both look at me, shrugging. The Priests say the prisoner caused a disturbance in the Temple, calling them traitors and collaborators — which, of course, they are — claiming they had desecrated the "house of The Lord God, his Father," whatever that means.

I gaze at the prisoner. I can see his anger about the High Priests, but they're useful to us. He must actually believe they should be devoted solely to the service of their god. A fanatic, then, but not of the sort they claim. I can see from where I sit that his own hands haven't labored over weapons or munitions. His long, slender fingers and alabaster skin are more like a woman's; his hands are more suitable for holding pen and ink — though I doubt he can read and write — than for assembling the swords, shields, and spears necessary for an army. He doesn't look like a warrior or Rebel or Zealot or a Freedom-Fighter. No, he looks like the teacher his followers and some of the others claim him to be.

A teacher, trying to return his people to their god.

But those eyes of his — oh, yes, I do see the spark that frightens them, the smoldering passion that makes them tremble.

That passion burning in his eyes is a fire for his god.

Yes, he burns, but not against the Roman Empire.

Perhaps he did attack some vendors in the Temple and claim the Priests have desecrated the "house of his Father." And so they have, with Roman collaboration.

All he did was speak the truth.

With one look he reduces them to a quivering mass because he forces them to see themselves. With one look from him, they fall against each other, their limbs jerking and twitching, their eyes rolling back, their lips frothing. Even my own legionnaires turn pale and tremble though he says not a word.

Brave man.

Foolish man.

Should I execute a man because he frightens others by making them see the truth about themselves?

If I look at him, will he make me see some truth about myself?

I wave the guard and the shopkeeper over to me.

"Ask him if he's plotting rebellion against the government?" I say to the guard in Roman, who asks the shopkeeper in *koinē*, who repeats the question to the prisoner in his own tongue.

He says nothing as his eyes continue to burn with that fire. But he does look up at me. It feels as if his hand is clenched around my heart. I glance down at the charges until I can catch my breath.

Rebellion, Treason, Tax Evasion, Terrorism, Inciting Riots.

"Have they so angered you by violating your god's temple that you would allow them to charge you with treason against the Roman Empire, though you've committed no such crime?"

That look comes back to his face, that pressure to my chest, and while the shopkeeper and the guard wait for his answer, which I know will never come, I realize that he's committed to throw himself under the hooves, to be crushed under the wheels, as if that will somehow stop the desecration, as if somehow he's been born to it, as if somehow his death will change things, and that — above all — what I do matters little to him.

It's a pity. But what can I do to stop him? We cannot even speak to each other. He wants me to sign. His eyes tell me that. I pick up the pen, dip it into the ink, and sign the death warrant.

So. There it is.

When I push aside the document, I see that there is a mark, a stain of some sort on my palm, and I rub my hand against my robe as they lead him away to the same end as all the others. I send one of the boys for water and towels. When he returns, I wash my hands. The water is cool and clear.

After I leave the palace and board my litter, I notice that my hand is still stained. I rub it against my robe, over and over. Lucius has left documents for me. I'll whip him when I see him next. I kick the documents out of my way, each headed with the traditional and usual notation: *To Our Most Honorable and Noble Prefect, Pontius Pilatus.*

Just as his was before I signed it.

And after.

His eyes are there when I close mine in the litter, leaving the city. His silence is heavy on my skin. A savage cry rips at me from the place they call *Golgotha* — Hill of Skulls — outside the city walls. Chosen by us long ago so every one of them can see the consequences of resisting us. A hill covered with crosses. Covered with the bones of their leaders. I let the litter-curtain fall into place.

A cloud passes, for a moment, in front of the sun.

The mark in my hand burns and burns.

Passion Play

"Why did you choose me?" I say.

"I needed you," he says.

"And now you don't?"

"I need you more than ever."

"If it weren't for me, you'd have lived your whole life in the desert with no one to worship you."

"Perhaps."

"All I've done for you, do I get even one word of thanks?"

"Thank you," he says, standing there with his unblinking eyes and a frayed rope in his hands, but I don't laugh.

"I'm not doing it," I say.

"You have to," he says, "or no one will believe you're grieving."

I cross my arms and give him a hard look.

"What else haven't told me?"

He just looks down at his feet. The rope dangles like a whip.

"You don't want your children to be ashamed of you, do you?"

"I'll tell you what I want," I say to him, grabbing that dirty rope out of his hands. "I want you to play by the rules."

"I am."

"Then why do the rules keep changing?"

I kick the sand, not caring that some of it goes into his face.

"You're the one I trust," he says. "Could I ask any of the others?"

"Every time we have it all worked out, you change things."

"That's because it's hard to know the best way. I've never done this before either."

I slam the coiled rope against a tree.

"This will be the last thing I ever ask you to do for me," he says.

❀

"Why didn't you tell me before?"

"I just thought of it."

"Who are you to say when someone lives or dies?"

"I'm doing it, too," he says.

"But you want me to jump out of a tree with a rope around my neck."

"Not till afterward."

"After you."

"Then people will feel sorry for you, too."

"I'm sorry for myself now, for listening to you all these years."

"You're the only one I trust with this."

"Why don't you do the rope," I say, "and I'll do the wood?"

"You don't mean that."

"If we're both going to end up the same way, what difference does it make who does rope and who does wood?"

"You know."

"Tell me again."

❀

He looks and looks at me with those eyes of his until the words run out of me, until my arms and legs grow heavy, until the wind blows sand in our hair and eyes, until it tugs at our clothes.

And still he looks at me.

"This is the last thing I'm doing for you," I say, throwing the rope down to the ground. "The very last thing, and this time, I mean it."

"Judas," he says, taking me in his arms and kissing me on each cheek. "My dear, sweet Judas."

Treason of the Blood

I'm not the one who balances her bare foot on the raised sleeping platform as she leans forward to adjust the clasp on one of her ankle bracelets, her head tilted so all her hair falls over one shoulder except for a strand or two near her full mouth, her silk skirt dragged up over her knee to reveal her taut thigh. I'm not the one who wets her lips with her tongue as she looks at me from under half-closed lids tinted violet and blue. I won't be to blame if he can't keep her satisfied.

Why, he blushes like a boy when we're sitting in the courtyard talking and she hugs him from behind, her arms around his shoulders, her lips to his ear, her breasts round and soft against the back of his head and neck. Some of the other men blush, too. None of the other women followers act like that. They listen to what he has to say. They speak to him, just as the men do. She's not thinking of any of that. She's only thinking of one thing, but he's too inexperienced for her. I could satisfy that mouth of hers. I could show her things he's never even dreamed of.

But I don't. He's my best friend.

He depends on me to keep the books so he can do his work. He needs me to watch over the others so he can concentrate on his dreams.

He trusts me not to touch her when she leans over me to place the dish of cucumbers and yogurt on the dining rug at supper though her breasts brush my shoulder and arm.

He trusts me to be faithful to him although I'm not the one who creeps over to my side of the sleeping platform in the middle of the night when he's away and says, "I'm lonely: would you hold me? Only for a little while."

And I'm not the one who bathes in the middle of the afternoon in the main room without a cloth to hide her nakedness were someone to walk in.

I'm not the one who looks at me in the glass as she colors her pale face, her sheer gown slipping off one perfumed shoulder, her painted mouth opening, round and full and moist as she sighs and whispers, "Yes, what is it? Just tell me what you want, my dear sweet Judas."

When the Dancer Is the Dance

O body swayed to music, O brightening glance,
How can we know the dancer from the dance?

William Butler Yeats
"Among School Children"

"It's too dangerous."

"I'm the one doing the dangerous part," he says.

"If they catch me helping you," I say, "they'll kill me where I stand, so I'm doing dangerous, too."

"That's why I'm counting on you. You're the only one brave enough..."

"You mean, stupid enough."

"Brave enough. Cunning enough."

❀

He'll never be able to convince me to go along with this scheme because this time, if we fail, men die. This plan isn't like what we pulled off in the Temple. That was so easy he could've done that by himself. We did the Temple the same as our other jobs. While he makes his way to the money, the boys and I guard the exits, to discourage heroism.

Once each of us is stationed, he storms through the place like he's an entire legion of foot soldiers, ranting while he's emptying the till. I've never seen anyone so magnificent. People scream, run, and cower on the floor; money, jewelry, and valuables roll everywhere — it's the greatest thing I've ever seen. When he struts about in the midst of the chaos, barking at people, ordering them to choose "God or money, God or money," grabbing them by the throat if they don't answer quickly enough — it's like seeing the face of God Himself. Nothing moves me like seeing him work.

The poor souls who have to make the choice are so terrified, he might as well tell them to choose between breathing and being buried alive. The ones who don't soil themselves or pass out usually drop to his feet and cover their heads with their hands and arms. He puts his foot on the backs of their necks — everyone knows who's the main attraction in his show.

The men claim they're having heart attacks, the women sob, but no one gets hurt. Even in the Temple job, no one got hurt.

That's why this new plan bothers me so much.

It can't be done without someone getting hurt.

Without someone getting killed.

❀

I should've known something was happening with the Temple job. I mean, there we were, with all this money and jewelry, but when we start to pick it up, he tells us to put it down. The boys are more than taken aback by this, yet when they question him, he says, "Man cannot serve two masters." Like any of us knows what that means.

He loses quite a few of the boys after that, and most of the others are less eager to go along with his plans. In fact, only a few of us are still completely loyal to him, myself included. At least, until what he does with the food.

Now that is beyond strange.

It's after the Temple, so a lot of the boys are already wondering when we're going to see some tangible reward for all our work. A split is already forming in the group. Then he does this thing with the food, and it changes everything.

❀

The gig starts in the usual way. He's in the center, giving the people the standard line, while the boys and I are working the crowd. It's a pretty big group, even for him, so his rep must be getting bigger, which is good. But then he starts throwing in some beatitudes he's never done before, which is not such a good idea on such a hot afternoon.

The crowd gets restless — hot, hungry, thirsty. They gripe, they shove each other, they shout things like, "When do we do something besides talk?"

Instead of getting the hint to cut it and head out, he asks them, "What is it you want?"

Some smart-mouth yells back, "Lunch."

There's a big rumble of laughter at that, and laughter's not exactly good for our cause, especially when it's not happy laughter. A couple of the boys come running over to me. They're worried about getting stoned, which is not an idle worry considering what that crowd of vipers in the valley did to us a few months ago.

From the middle of the crowd, standing above everyone else on account of that slight hill, he holds up a basket.

"My friends will distribute this food," he says. "Behold how I take care of my own."

The boys and I get up to him fast. We're probably all wondering how to get him out of there without any of us getting maimed or killed, and the boys look like they're thinking of dragging him back to the Highlands and naming a new leader. When we get to him, he reaches into the basket, pulls out some bread, fish, and wine. He tells us to give it out as fast as we can if we want to live to see tomorrow. So we do.

Now, here's the frightening part. No matter how many times we go back to the basket, it's never emptied. This hugely big crowd eats and eats and drinks till their fat bellies get even fatter, till their bellies are so full they want to take naps, till we get plenty of new members signed up with cash contributions without any rough stuff or coercion or anything, that's how content they're feeling.

And this is the even stranger part: there's enough food left over in the basket for our dinner that night.

❀

I don't even know how he did it, and I usually know how he does everything, and I mean everything. The boys are spooked, I can tall you. They don't want to follow a magician or a sorcerer or, worse yet, a devil. Some of them don't even eat supper that night. They don't want anything to do with that food. They sneak off to go back to their families.

I'm a little scared myself, and I have to tell you, even the Lord God Himself doesn't frighten me. I figure there has to be a logical explanation for it. Maybe he picked up some of the Temple money. Maybe that's how he pulled off the food thing.

But the Temple job and the food trick — they're nothing compared to what he wants to do now. Someone's going to get killed this time, and once someone dies, the authorities will be all over these hills looking for us — if they're not already — and if they find us, it won't matter if we've left the group of not. It'll be guilt — and death — by association. That's why I'm so anxious about this scheme of his.

❀

"This will get everyone to join us," he says.

"So they can be hunted down like the rest of us?" I say.

"Don't be so pessimistic."

"This is *not* going to work."

"I'm telling you, it is."

"No..."

"We'll do it on a Sabbath. The bodies have to be removed by sunset, so you'll be waiting there and just before sunset..."

"Waiting where, exactly?"

"Somewhere close by."

"Close by what?"

"Me, of course."

"That means, close by the guards."

"I know that."

"They don't let anyone near the condemned."

"I know that, too."

"So, how am I going to be waiting 'close by'?"

He glances toward the hill, by the city walls.

"You could wait there, where the hill is higher than the walls," he says. "Walk over the wall onto the hill."

"What if they don't put you near the wall?"

"Are you going to hear me out or not?"

"No. Because I'm not doing this."

"Without you, none of it works."

"You mean, without me, you die."

He presses his fingers to his forehead as if he has a great pain in his head. After he opens his eyes, he gazes over the wall and the hill instead of at me. He rubs his neck, leans his head back and turns it from side to side, stretches his shoulders. When he looks at me again, I realize how different he seems.

❀

"I'm not doing it."

"The guards on duty will be tired. They'll want to go home. Some of them always leave before the next group arrives."

"Can you not hear me tonight?" I say. "I'm not doing it."

"You can bribe any of the guards who don't leave. They'll think I'm dead..."

"This isn't some game we're playing."

"I have enough money for you to bribe however many guards are there..."

"Will you listen to yourself? You've gone mad."

"I won't really die. You'll get me before then. But you and I will be the only ones who know that I didn't really die."

"I'm not doing it. One mistake, one stubborn guard, one honest legionnaire, and you're really dead. Listen to me, will you?"

He leans forward, puts his hand on mine, and lowers his voice to a whisper.

"Everyone else will think I died on that cross and came back from the dead. It's the ultimate miracle. Don't you see? They'll think God Himself saved me. We'll be able to overthrow the Romans without any weapons at all."

❀

My body and soul are wracked with fear when he explains how he'll refuse the myrrh sometimes offered on a dampened sponge to the crucified to make them sleep, to relax their arms and legs so they can't fight, to let them die more quickly. He'll refuse the bitter myrrh, he tells me, to better feign death. My body quakes when he instructs me which tools to use to take the iron spikes out of his wrists and ankles. I grow cold when he describes the quickest way to the Galilean Highlands, where we'll hide for three days. I want to retch when his voice quickens as he describes his triumphal entry back into Jerusalem, when his eyes glow as he details how the populace will

81

revere him, when he holds his head up as if he already wore a crown and wielded a scepter.

For the first time since I've known him, I don't understand him at all. When he grips my forearm, it feels like a serpent wrapping its cold, tightly muscled body around me, paralyzing me, dragging me down with him. He leans so close to my ear I can feel his lips brush my skin.

"As long as you're not late, this will work."

"You haven't thought this through well enough."

"I know what I'm doing," he says.

I shake my head, but he keeps whispering in that voice he uses sometimes, that voice that tugs you into his visions, that voice that makes you do things against your own God-given free will.

"Trust me, Judas," he says. "Just trust me."

Slaying the Dragon

Then another sign appeared in heaven...
The dragon was enraged... and went off to make war.

Revelations 12:3, 12:17

*E*ach time it takes longer for me to reach the wall: the cave's intricate mazes constantly change. Panting, sweating, the rock wall cold against my back, the bonfire of the red dragon's seven heads bear down on me, each head with its ten horns and seven crowns. My eyelashes, brows, and the hair on my forearms are singed away from the heat. I can't hold my sword to fight him off, I can't breathe, I'm trapped. My stomach heaves, and my heart pounds so fast that I begin to collapse from dizziness and exhaustion. He wants war, but surely he realizes that I have no means to fight him.

Why doesn't he just end it by destroying me?

Then I wake.

My wife says I deserve the great red dragon, though she wasn't always so callous. In the beginning, she held me in her arms, stroked my face or hair, murmured in my ear, soothed me back to sleep.

Soon, she became irritable. She sighed loudly and turned away from me in the bed. She pulled the coverings over her head.

"This is a huge house," she said. "With many bedrooms."

"Meaning?"

"Why don't you pick another *cubiculum*?"

"Another?"

"If you can't get any sleep in your own *cubiculum,* there are plenty of others for you to choose from."

"Guest rooms."

She sat up.

"This dragon is clearly a punishment."

"What?"

"The gods have sent it."

"You don't believe in the gods," I said.

"Of course, I do."

"Since when?"

"Since we came to this place."

"I don't believe in them," I said, getting out of the bed that we used to share far more often than we do now.

"Whether you believe in them or not, you have to pay."

"For what?"

"Your crime."

"*My* crime?"

She crossed her arms over her chest, looked at me through narrowed eyes. I spread my hands apart, my mouth open, my shoulders slumped as she put on her lavish bed-robe. She stepped into her night-shoes before she wrapped a silk shawl around her shoulders. She didn't kiss me before she left the room.

What crime have I ever committed? Accepting monetary favors? Giving coin to persuade stubborn but influential men? Keeping my portion of the allotted taxes? Giving informants coin for valuable knowledge?

Everyone does those things.

How could she possibly accuse me of committing any crimes? After all our years together, how could she treat me this way? Not many men in my position treat their wives as well as I do her; they don't treat their mistresses as well as I do my wife. I've never even taken a lover, let alone kept a mistress, though it's the custom. I even stayed with her after it became clear that she would never give me children, and I could've publicly repudiated her for that. No one would've blamed me either.

Yet now my wife abandons me. Betrays me. Accuses me of being a criminal.

I stood there a few moments, ready to march into whatever *cubiculum* she'd chosen for the night, to tell her exactly how angry I was. Yes, I thought as I strode across the room and flung aside the sheer curtains covering the opening, I'd show her who was the master in this house.

I stopped, surrounded by the fire of the great red dragon. I turned in every direction, looking for the glint of his golden crowns in the twilight of the hall as I shouted for a weapon. My guards were there instantly, encircling me, their backs to me, their swords and shields out to defend me. A strange mist floated across the marble floor and over the rain-water pool — dragon's breath.

"Do you see that?" I said.

"See what, Sir?"

"There, on the floor, by your ankles."

They looked down, then at each other.

"If we follow it, we can catch it."

"Catch what, Sir?"

Their confused expressions paralyzed me for a moment.

"Oh, by the gods, I took too much wine at dinner," I said. "I must have been walking in my dreams. Go, go. I'm fine. Fine."

I went to my own bedroom and let my body fall backward. I was chilled. I pulled the bedclothes around me. There was no mist around me, no cave walls, no seven heads with burning blasts. The dragon wasn't in my room because I was awake, and he only came in dreams.

I realized, however, that my wife was right. The great red dragon had declared war on me.

And I already knew my crime.

I'd knowingly condemned an innocent man to death.

⚜

I haven't forgotten any of it though I like to pretend I have. If I drink enough, I actually don't remember — for a while. But he always comes back, my *Innoceo*, like a lover who can't forget me.

He was charged with treason, terrorism, tax evasion, plotting to overthrow the government, inciting riots. The man who stood before me was no Rebel, no Terrorist, no Anarchist. There was no blood on his hands. There was probably no blood on the hands of his followers. He seemed meek. None of his followers had been captured: that proved their cowardice. At least to me.

His enemies were the powerful ones. They'd drawn up the charges against him. I don't remember why I was even in court. I rarely sat on the bench then. I was too powerful to have to deal with trials. I had standing orders for the only crimes that even required my signature, and my aide signed those documents most of the time. Only capital punishment crimes required death by crucifixion: Rebellion, Insurrection, and Assassination of government-appointed officials.

He wasn't guilty of any of those.

His eyes gave him away.

When the prosecutor read the charges, they were so preposterous. He may have been a fanatic, but he was more a religious fanatic than a Zealot. With his long unkempt hair and raggedy beard, he looked like those doom-sayers who've been plaguing us for years — the ones who give away their possessions, quit their wives and family, abandon personal hygiene and modest clothing, publicly practice flagellation, roam the countryside predicting the annihilation of most humans, and call down their God's wrath on everyone except themselves.

There was one, years ago, named John, called The Baptizer. One of the local officials despised him. It seems that John used to stand outside the official's house and shout obscenities at the official because he'd married his former sister-in-law. By the gods, she hated The Baptizer with a ferocity that would have made her a formidable gladiator or legionnaire. I don't know why The Baptizer John cared that they'd married. After all, she'd divorced his brother, so what was the problem?

But, you see, I digress, as my wife claims I always do when I'm forced to think of my *Innoceo*...

❀

He was different from the other prophets, teachers, and healers — even the most devout of them. I sensed it the moment we looked at each other. The entire time the prosecution was presenting its case against him, I knew he wasn't guilty. Not of the crimes he was accused of. Terrorism? Inciting riots? Military rebellion? Tax evasion? No, not him.

I gave him the chance to defend himself. I offered to delay the proceedings, to appoint him a representative and a proper translator. He simply stared at me. I'd found a guard who'd been stationed there long enough to have become fluent in the prisoner's own language. No matter what I asked, the prisoner wouldn't answer.

By not denying or refuting the charges, he silently told me, in effect, that he wished to die.

I merely acquiesced, you might say.

I simply granted his wish to commit suicide.

❀

My wife says it's not that clear-cut. My moral obligation, according to her, was to delay the hearing and the execution until the man realized what effect his silence would have. When I insist that he understood perfectly the consequences of his behavior, she gets into a rage, and insists that the dragon-dreams are my punishment for sending a man I knew to be innocent to a painful and shameful death.

She believes I deserve to suffer.

For the rest of my life.

My wife doesn't respect or pity me anymore, and, as if the dragon with his seven heads, ten horns, and seven crowns weren't enough to battle every night, my *Innoceo* haunts me every minute that I do not sleep.

❀

I turn the corner in the marketplace, bumping into one of these people who know they're supposed to stay out of my way, and I see his eyes.

A child wearing a crown of woven branches plays king in the corner of the marketplace, and the crown of thorns dig into my *Innoceo*'s forehead and scalp, leaving rivulets of dark blood in his hair and on his face.

I hear a group of their women wailing like they do, and he's on the cross again, surrounded by women — his wife, his mother, some of his female followers, I don't know who they all were — and I'm hiding in the shadows again or crouching behind the city wall, for days, waiting for him to die, praying to gods I don't believe in, praying to his god whose name I don't even know, praying to any god for it all to just be over so that he won't have to suffer any longer.

And I have to crouch in some alley until the weeping is over, the weeping that is as great as it was each day and night as I waited for him to die, knowing that I was the one who killed him.

Is that not punishment enough?

I requested to return home, thinking the dragon couldn't survive outside its desert. I heard that after Caesar read my petition, he let it fall to the floor, laughing.

For the first time in my entire career, I've nothing to say on my behalf. For the first time in my life, I've been struck dumb. For the first time in his entire life, the great and powerful Pontius Pilate, *Prefect* of Judaea, has absolutely no weapon with which to slay the greater and more powerful dragon sent by their god to avenge His *Innoceo*.

Part Four

Stay, you imperfect speakers: tell me more.

Shakespeare
Macbeth 1.3.70

Speaking in Tongues

*A*llow me to be frank — you wish to know how I came to be with him, why I stayed with him, and how I felt about him after I discovered the... truth. That's the wound everyone wishes to probe. It's people like you, my dear, who've caused my feelings for him to become a wound, then prevented the wound from healing. That's why you're here, isn't it? To probe the wound.

Among other things?

Ah, you're clever.

What? Dinner's ready? Yes, set an extra plate. No, no, I insist that you stay. My wife loves having guests. I must warn you, though, she doesn't like it when this subject is brought up. You know, you're exactly like all the others who've climbed this mountain and sought an answer to the very same question: Did I love him?

I spent twenty years in prison for him.

Isn't that love?

My wife doesn't like the term "love" when it's applied to him. She prefers "obsession." Don't be absurd, Gretel. That's why she's come. To hear the truth. Obsession, adoration, love. Does it matter what we call it? Of course I prefer the word "love" or "admiration" since I believe those words most accurately depict my feelings for him.

I'm not an emotional man. Still, I never doubted my love for him. I never hid my feelings. He was the greatest... the most... it's so complicated to explain to someone as young as you.

Were you even alive then?

No, I didn't think so.

Why don't you simply ask me the questions you have written down on your tablet and let me answer them? All right, let's begin.

Did I continue to love him during those twenty years I spent in prison for him? Obviously. It's not in my nature to be unfaithful.

Please, don't embarrass my wife or make me angry by questioning me about that. I'm well aware of the claims that there was an *erotic* component to my love for him, and to his for me. Such claims are ridiculous.

Was there what? *A repressed homosexual component to our love?* I really must insist that you apologize to my wife. *Homosexual, erotic, non-sexual homo-erotic.* It's ludicrous. He was a mentor, a father-figure, a friend. Yes, a friend. I'm not ashamed to say it. No, no matter how many people died because of him. You seem to forget: we were at war...

But we were talking about friendship. I was the closest thing he had to a friend. Love between friends, my dear young girl, is neither homosexuality nor eroticism.

Is the roast beef to your liking? Good. Actually, I prefer mine slightly more rare, but my wife was trying not to interrupt us. Here, do have more potatoes — Margret makes this dish especially well.

What's your next question? Did any of those men in his inner circle notice... I must insist that we not lend credence to this absurd accusation by continually using words such as *erotic*. No, you haven't offended me at all; I simply wanted to clarify... .

I beg your pardon. I wasn't aware that I'd raised my voice. Yes, you warned me that you would be asking some difficult questions. Yes, I did agree to answer them. However, if we're to have a working relationship, I don't want to continually spar over semantics.

Yes, that *is* much more satisfactory.

Yes, the men in his inner circle did, indeed, notice our "special" relationship. I was in his cabinet, after all. They noticed, and they were jealous of me.

Should I have cared what the rest of his inner circle thought of me? Cutthroats and traitors, all of them. Even before the surrender, most of them had betrayed him by offering evidence and testimony in return for their own worthless lives. Treacherous lies from self-serving mouths.

I never betrayed him. My name wasn't among those of the assassins. I know my name was on that list discovered in the safe, but I'm sure you know there was a question mark beside my name.

Even then, they realized I'd never betray him.

Ah, you are, indeed, well prepared. Yes, I did consider assassinating him myself. Later on. But I was relieved when circumstances prevented it. I don't see how it could be called betrayal, my dear, if I myself chose not to carry it out. It was merely a moment of... how shall I describe it... disillusionment — yes, that's what it was — disillusionment with some of his political decisions, not disillusionment with him personally.

&

As you can see from the look on her face, my wife doesn't like my sense of humor. Margret doesn't like to discuss the past at all, do you, my dear Gretel? Why don't you get us another bottle of wine? Yes, that one's fine: give me the corkscrew.

Not only was disobeying his direct orders *not* a betrayal, it was actually a noble act, considering his state of mind at the time. I don't know the answer to that question, of course: one can never be sure if he was mad toward the end. I suspect he may have been extremely close to madness. Does one stop loving another simply because his reason has fled?

With dessert, we'll have a special, sweet wine. You'll like it. And Margret made *apfelkuchen* — apple cake. You must have some.

Was it madness or the war that affected his behavior at the end? I suppose we'll never know, will we?

Yes, I know I've been credited with extending the war. When they attribute my extending the war to my efficiency and diligence, they're not complimenting me, are they? Should I be damned because I was efficient and diligent, or should I be damned because I loved him?

I am, indeed, damned, Gretel. Surely even you don't believe that twenty years in prison is sufficient compensation for the destruction of millions of lives.

Yes, I do accept responsibility for the dead: I did so at my trial, though you're too young to remember that. *Mea culpa, mea culpa, mea maxima culpa:* that's what I said during my trial. Yes, "melodramatic" has been one of the accusations against me. Unlike many others, I'm not afraid of acknowledging my guilt.

I mean, our guilt, our collective guilt.

When you say "noble," I detect quite a bit of sarcasm.

I'm well aware that the younger generation has been burdened with the guilt and responsibility for their parents' behavior.

No, the sins of the fathers should not be visited upon their children.

❀

You see how Margret's face changes at the prospect of discussing the children. This is what Margret exists for — kitchen, church, children. What? You know that phrase? Such an old saying, yet you've heard of it. You must read a very great deal to be familiar with that. No, I'm not embarrassing Margret in the least. She loves talking about the children. As for me, it's as if she's relating news about strangers. I doubt that she's shocked, Gretel. She knows I spent twenty years in prison, twenty years that my children grew up without me.

I imagine the children are already aware of my feelings… Very well, my *lack* of feelings for them. It certainly *is* reciprocal. Don't lie, Gretel. I'm being honest. Margret was the only parent the children had most of their lives. Even before prison, I was so involved with the war…

You're very blunt, aren't you? One forgets how different young people are these days. It's true. It wasn't the war which made me a poor father. You're completely correct. It was my relationship with him that kept me away from my family, my relationship with him that made me a poor father and a poor husband.

I'm afraid I can't tell you what my children think of what I did: we don't talk. We become silent and uncomfortable in each other's presence. I can only infer their judgment of me, but I assume that it isn't a favorable one.

You needn't defend me, Gretel.

Do they love me? Ah, you see that my wife doesn't hurry to answer for me this time. To tell you the truth, I'd be astonished if someone told me that my children love me. The very least I can hope for is that they don't despise me.

Would you like sugar in your coffee? Cream?

❀

No, even my children wouldn't accuse me of that. They know I don't believe any one race superior to another. Those who accuse me of that are lying. My relationship with him was about our common interests, not about politics or racial issues.

For example? Drawing, architecture, and re-building the city.

You must believe me when I tell you that war changes one's perception, my dear. I never said it excuses one's actions, though it does change the way one views those actions. No, I never knew about those places and what was happening there until the trial. Not many of us did. Yes, I knew there were political prisoners — everyone knew that — but I had no idea they were being executed.

What's wrong with that word? Very well, then, since you object to "executed" — I had no knowledge that political prisoners were being killed. You object to that word as well? What word would you prefer?

Exterminated?

I never would have chosen that word myself...

Enough of this. You didn't come all the way here to talk about political prisoners. Why don't you just ask me what you really want to know?

What do *I* think you really want to know?

You want to ask me if I still loved him after I found out about them. I can see by the look on your face that I've guessed correctly. What's my answer?

Yes. Yes, I still loved him after I discovered what he'd done to them. Gretel, don't contradict me. She wants to hear the truth. Let me say it.

Yes, I loved him.

And, yes, I do love him still.

There. I've said it. Are you quite satisfied? I love him. Even now. And I've paid for it. With what? With twenty years of my life, in prison. I'm still paying for it, in here, where no one else can see it.

No one but me and God? Are you trying to show me that you have a sense of humor or are you mocking me?

No, of course you're not. Apology accepted.

Yes, I consider my own moral debt paid.

His, also.

How?

He died. Isn't that payment enough?

Whether you like to admit it or not, he's paid his debt, and, in my opinion, he's paid a far greater price than I did.

Homosexuality, betrayal, extermination — such words are ugly even when they come from the mouth of a pretty, young girl. Uglier, in fact. But I'm not avoiding anything. No, I'm not. I'm not being gallant either. I'm merely being honest. If we're to have a working relationship...

You have such a cynical smile for one so young. How did you become so cynical? Yes, of course, I understand. This is about me, not you.

Ah, more ugly words. If you're not careful, I'll forget how young and pretty you are. I'll become short-tempered. No, I'm not threatening you at all.

No, Gretel, we don't want any more *apfelkuchen.* Will you please stop interrupting us? Yes, more coffee is what we need. We'll take it in the study.

What? Already? Yes, we have been talking a long time today. I'm not tired. Ah, you've forgotten extra blank tapes. No, I haven't any. I suppose we will have to wait till tomorrow to continue. That's fine. I have nothing planned. Tomorrow at ten.

I'll show you some of my letters, and some of my unpublished manuscripts. I told you I would. The drafts of the published ones, too, if you wish.

It was a pleasure meeting you as well, my dear.

Please, do call me Albert.

Herr Speer sounds much too formal, too distant.

And I would so like us to become friends.

Sorry, Wrong Number, *Redux*

I can't believe you're telling me this over the phone. After all our time together, you didn't have the decency to tell me in person? What do you mean you've tried? When? Is that what you were trying to tell me? Then why did you let me... That's not true. We do not always end up in bed together. We spend time together without... Yes, we do. Plenty of times. No, *not* just when *I* was trying to end it. Wait... I think I heard the car. I have to go, Angela. You know I can't. I've told you. That just isn't how you end it with your wife of twenty years. I wouldn't expect you to understand. I've got to go. I'll call you later."

"Who was that?"

"No one. A wrong number. They hung up."

"I heard you talking."

"It was a wrong number, Barbara."

"Jeffrey, are you..."

"No, I'm not. Don't look at me like that. I learned my lesson the last time."

"You always say that."

"This time I mean it."

"Is that why you're standing so close to the liquor?"

"I need a drink."

"Have you looked in the mirror lately? You look like an old man. All that drinking and smoking is catching up with you."

"Shut up, why don't you? Get out of my way. I need a drink."

"You mean, you need a divorce."

"Could you please get away from the refrigerator door, Barbara? I need some ice."

"What makes the last time different from all the other times, Jeffrey?"

"You went to a lawyer. Whom I paid for, I might add."

"You mean that's all I had to do all these years to make you take your marriage vows seriously: go to a lawyer?"

"Barbara, how many times do we have to go through this? Are you going to make me do penance for the rest of my life? Here, let me help you put the groceries away. Don't look at me like that. I've helped you around the house plenty of times. Move. Please. I need to open that cupboard."

"That's not where the pasta goes, Jeffrey. It goes over here."

"When did you move it? What? What's the matter?"

"Aren't you going to answer the phone?"

"You're closer to it than I am, Barbara. You answer it."

"It's not for me."

"Let it ring, then. Hand me those vegetables. I'll put them away."

"She probably forgot to tell you something urgent, Jeffrey, like how she can't wait till you're in her bed again."

"Jesus, Barbara..."

"Don't slam the cupboards like that. You'll break the crystal."

"I'll slam the cupboard doors if I want to. It's my money that paid for the crystal in the first place, and if I want to break it, I will."

"That's all that's important to you, isn't it — money?"

"It's my money that pays for your fancy manicures and that highlighted hair of yours."

"Answer the phone, Jeffrey."

"You answer it."

"Hello? Hello?"

"Who was it?"

"She hung up."

"It must have been a wrong number. Just like I told you."

"You know, I'd respect you so much more it you just admitted you wanted out..."

"And lose half of everything I've worked for all these years? No, thank you."

"I've earned it, too."

"You've never worked a day in your life. I've always taken care of you."

"I've paid for it by putting up with you all these years."

"You've paid for it? *You've* paid for it? That's a laugh. Did you pay for this platinum-rimmed china? Or this Waterford crystal? I don't think so."

"It belongs to me more than it does to you."

"The hell it does."

"Oh, that's mature. Why don't you throw another glass?"

"I'll throw any goddamned thing I want to. It's my house. They're my glasses. It's my china, and if I want to break every single dish in this cupboard, I will."

"Oh, that's good. Break a few more plates, why don't you? I don't know why I put up with you. You're so damned melodramatic."

"Melodramatic? That's funny, Barbara, coming from..."

"Don't you dare touch me."

"I wasn't going to touch you. Why are you so paranoid?"

"If you ever hit me again, you'll lose more than half of what you own."

"I never hit you."

"Then how did I end up in the emergency room with broken ribs?"

"I wouldn't know. I'd been drinking. I don't know how you hurt yourself."

"There she is again, Jeffrey. You must be late for your rendezvous. Go on. Answer it. I dare you."

"Let go of my tie. It's a wrong number."

"Isn't it strange how we get these wrong number calls in cycles, like every time you start a new relationship. Where are you going?"

"Get out of my way, Barbara. Let go of me."

"Answer the phone."

"Get out of my way, I said."

"Let go of me. I told you not to touch me again."

"You push me too far, Barbara. You always do. And I've reached the end of my patience with you."

"You've reached the end of *your* patience? What about me? Do you think I like being married to a man who can't even satisfy a woman... you sonofa..."

"You asked for that, Barbara. What are you doing? Put that down. Damn it, Barbara — put that knife down. Barbara... Bar..."

"Hello? Yes. It's done. No. Completely done. Yes, I told you I could do it. No, he's not moving. All right, just a minute. No, he's not breathing. I did it just like you told me. Yes, he hit me. Several times. Hard enough that there'll be bruises. Yes, there's blood. I think he loosened a tooth, too. Yes, finally, after all these years. No, I'll call the police as soon as we hang up. What did you say to him when you called? You didn't? Over the phone? That was brilliant. Yes, darling, now we get everything. Just the two of us. Stupid bastard. That noise? I just kicked him. He deserved more than that. Yes, I'll call you as soon as I can. Remember, now: you called a second time since the two of you got interrupted the first time, and I answered again, but we didn't talk, of course. You said nothing, so I finally hung up. Yes, darling, I know. Me, too. I'll call you in a day or two. We can be together then, just like we planned. Yes, Angela, darling, I love you, too. You know I do."

Hunchback of the Midwest

I'm a freak: I admit it. But every woman I've ever met has succumbed to the power of my great, humped back. So I'm not to blame for anything that happened. They loved me. Was I *not* supposed to love them in return?

The first woman who couldn't keep her hands off was my mother, Belle. Mothers are supposed to touch their children, but what Belle did wasn't ordinary touching. From what she says, Belle didn't want to touch me at all, at first, and therein lay the problem. Belle tried to raise me without coming into contact with my humped back. She claims she never held me when I was an infant, no matter how I bawled, but by the time I was four or five, my back must've overpowered her because she was touching me all the time.

"Don't look at me like that," said Belle. "How many times do I have to tell you? Don't look at me."

I always tried to stare at my dinner plate, but she was so beautiful that I wanted to gaze at her forever, and dinner was usually cabbage or potatoes or onions congealed in grease. Belle was terrified to let me eat meat: she feared it might make my back grow. I'd stare at the plate for a few minutes before my eyes would stray back to gaze on the glory of Belle.

"Why aren't you eating? Eat," she said. "Are you deformed *and* deaf?"

I knew Belle was exhausted from her hard day bent over a sewing machine. She emptied her glass of beer and stretched her aching back to cross the kitchen to get another. After those long hours over the machine, her back was almost as curved as mine, and she mumbled as she opened the refrigerator.

"If it hadn't been for you, Vincent, I'd have made something of my life," she said, night after night, until it became a litany. "I'd have been somebody, Vincent. I'd have been somebody."

Belle never told me what she would've been if it hadn't been for the misfortune of my unplanned birth and the greater misfortune of my deformity, which, according to her, had driven my father from us. If she'd told me, I might've had the opportunity to make it up to her.

Suddenly, she would be behind me, her breath hot in my ear.

"If you had to be a freak, why couldn't you have been born with a tail?" she said. "At least we could've cut a tail off, or hidden it in your trousers."

I had to get out of her way fast, before she touched my back. Belle believed I should elude her when she was overcome by the urge to touch my hump. Sometimes, I did manage to get out of the way, but mostly, I didn't. It wouldn't have mattered. Belle was obsessed with my hump, and she could never satisfy her need to touch it. So touch it she did, with a ferocity that left me cowering in the corner. After each bruising encounter, Belle would retreat to her bedroom, where she'd stay for days.

Those times, despite the ache in my hump from Belle's attention, were worth the discomfort because when Belle barricaded herself in her room, I didn't have to go down to the basement, a place I abhorred, with its dark smelly dampness, its strange noises, its spiders. While Belle was shut up in her room, I didn't have to sleep in my crib in the basement. I could sleep on the couch or on the floor or even on the kitchen table if I wanted.

The longing for Belle always returned, however, and one morning I'd be sitting on the floor outside her room, thumb in my mouth, head against the doorframe. Belle opened the door. She didn't seem to mind my looking at her then. She'd sweep me up into her arms, hug me to her perfumed breast, and lavish me with kisses as she wept tears of repentance. I always forgave her. It wasn't so simple for Belle. She was never able to forgive me for being a freak, although, with her last breath, she confessed how much she loved me, so I'm able to remember those years with Belle as happy.

My mother wasn't the only woman affected by this humped back. Before the end of grammar school, the beautiful Diana proved herself susceptible. Ah, Diana. Goddess of the sixth grade, goddess of the cheerleading squad, goddess of my life. I was desperately, madly in love. I sneaked into the gym every day after school to watch her practice. The other cheerleaders ran away when they saw me sit down under the bleachers, but not Diana.

Oh, she stared into the distance as if she didn't notice me, and got a look on her face identical to Belle's, and she sometimes openly admired the male athletes working with weights in my presence, but those things merely inflamed my ardor. Diana sensed rather than saw me, just as I detected her cherry-scented lip-gloss whenever she came anywhere near. After the other girls had run out of the gymnasium, Diana sighed, hands on her hips, blue-and-white pompoms dangling by her thighs.

"I know you're under there, Vincent," she said, moving a few steps away as my poor heart hammered. "Fine. Don't answer me."

I always slipped out from under the bleachers before she took another step. If I was good, I got to carry her school-bag to her house and creep with her into the garage. It was cool and shadowy. Because her parents worked, no one was home. Diana closed the door of the empty garage while I positioned myself in the center of the floor. I stood deathly still, even stiller than I ever had for Belle.

In the garage, the goddess of my life walked around and around and around, getting closer and closer to me with each circle, her pompoms *swish swish swishing* with each step. I made myself stare rigidly ahead, for once she'd caught me looking at her and made me go home without my reward.

Sometimes, as I stood there trembling in that cool and pungent dark, awaiting that first touch, I thought those slow circles would never end, but they always did. Finally my sweet Diana would be near enough for those beautiful blue-and-white pompoms to brush against my hump. How they made me shudder. Diana tapped me on the shoulder: that was the command to remove my shirt. *Swish swish swish* went the pompoms over my bare back. Her fingers brushed me.

The first time she touched my naked skin, I was so excited, I couldn't help myself: I cried out when it happened. It repulsed Diana so much that she swore on her dead dog's grave she'd never come near me again. I begged, wept, knelt, swore on my mother's grave not to let that vile thing happen in her presence again. Only then did the beautiful Diana relent and allow me back into Paradise.

Oh, sweet Diana. Sometimes she explored the terrain of my hump with her fingertips, sometimes with the back of her hand, sometimes her fingernails. Once she tested my hump with pins, a few times with a lit cigarette, and once with a hammer. Mostly, though, the beautiful Diana examined me with her tongue. Oh, the memory of it enflames me still. How she rewarded me for my patient subservience while she had her way with my hump. After she'd satisfied her own desires, she allowed me one chaste, close-mouthed kiss. What ecstasy, to bear the strokes, pricks, and kisses of such a goddess. I would've suffered vast torments merely to be fondled by the lovely Diana. How did I know then that even greater joy was yet to be mine?

One day my goddess wanted to determine if her nibbles and licks on my humped back had any effect on another part of my anatomy. Oh, joy. Complete and utter joy. I wanted nothing other than to be her slave forever, and perhaps I would've been if Diana's mother hadn't come home sick from work and spied her daughter swallowing the forbidden fruit, my fists clenched in ecstasy and my muscled arms raised in unspeakable satisfaction, just as Diana's mother opened the garage door to park the car.

Alas, the day I was driven from the Garden. Alas, the day I was forced to cover my hump with metaphorical fig leaves and go, lonely and alone, out into the wilderness. Even Adam was permitted to take his Eve. Not so with Vincent and his beautiful Diana. My maternal aunt and uncle hid me on their farm in another state while Diana's family set a great marble angel with his flaming sword at the gate of Paradise. Oh, cruelty beyond belief. Punishment beyond the crime. Alas, no mercy for poor, innocent Vincent, who'd never even tasted the forbidden fruit himself.

Though I ran away from the farm as soon as I could, rattled the iron chains on the bars, and roared in vain at the great stone angel standing in silent vigil over my Diana, she was kept forever from me.

For years I searched for another Diana. Loreena from Kansas City, Margaret from Green River, Janice from Columbia. Each was satisfactory in her own way, and each became a part of me, but none lit my flame as Diana had. Then, most unexpectedly, and to my greatest surprise, the flame of my fairest Diana flickered and sputtered in a great pool of wax. Extinguished by the brilliant, eclipsing light of Elena.

✤

Oh, Elena, Elena. Even the pen trembles at your memory. The breeze sighs your name. Stars form a crown for your dark hair, but those stars dim beside the ethereal glow of your eyes and face. Oh, Elena, my Elena, did I breathe before you gazed at me? Did I live before you smiled at me? Did my poor, lonely heart beat before I knew the touch of your hand? Say the very name *Elena* and my back rises and swells. Say the name *Elena* and I lose myself. I'm not responsible for what happens. Oh, sweet, darling Elena. How I loved you. And how you tormented me. Elena was the only woman in my entire life who wouldn't touch my back.

Elena even used my back as the excuse for not sleeping in the same bed as me. She was terrified my poor hump might brush against her in the dark. I offered to sleep with my shirt on, place a pillow between us, sleep on the floor beside her bed like a dog beside its master, but she was too skittish to agree to any of it.

Elena was the most magnificent woman I've ever known. Oh, the things she did to me. Even I could never have imagined them. If only she'd touched my hump, how happy I would've been. Everything in life would've been perfect. The way to the Garden, long barred, would've opened again before us, and angels themselves would've escorted us inside.

But Elena would not touch my back. I pleaded, threatened, bribed and cursed, to no avail. Her resistance was formidable. My passion and obsession grew in proportion to her obstinacy.

Finally, one night, maddened beyond endurance, I used force.

After all these years, it shames me still.

My back was determined to triumph, and triumph it did. Elena's spirit crumpled under the force of my back's determination. Our relationship buckled and collapsed under the strain of my back's desire. Our love dried to a fine dust and was scattered in the wind.

If only regret were wine, and I could drink myself to forgetfulness.

For days after I lost Elena, I stood on that fateful bridge and wept out my repentance. For weeks, as punishment, I kept my back away from women, locking myself in my rented room at night, with nothing but my records and my books. For months I roamed the riverbank, searching for Elena's body, until finally the police drove me away on the supposition that, deranged by grief, I would follow my lovely Elena to her watery grave. I wanted merely to find her body before they did, to hold her one last time, to beg her forgiveness.

All this was long ago; it's more like a dream than part of my life. Elena was the only woman I ever loved. For Elena, I would've taken the knife to my own back, but by the time I realized that, it was too late. She'd left me behind.

Oh, how I've repented. How I've grieved. When I was younger, lying on the floor in Belle's cold, damp basement, I thought I couldn't live without Belle, but I did. When I was driven from Diana, I thought I'd surely die, yet somehow I survived. I thought I couldn't survive without Elena, but here I am. I never would've imagined that I could live here, like this, in a cage, yet I do.

It's not so bad here, really, though sometimes when I wake in the night, the bars make me think I'm back in my crib in the basement, and my heart thuds so that I can't catch my breath. It's not so bad here, though they insist on calling me *Vincenzo*: the boss doesn't want the customers to know I was born of an ordinary woman like Belle, in Dubuque. When Bill the Goat Boy told me that my full name, advertised on the posters and billboards, was *Vincenzo Quasimodo*, I laughed to think how few would appreciate the allusion.

It's not too bad, not too lonely. Anyone with a quarter can come up to reach through the bars to touch my back, and it doesn't cost any extra if they make a wish. True, some of the men are rough, and I have to rattle the bars and bare my teeth so they step back. The women and children are gentle. If I turn my head while they're touching me, their eyes widen and their breath gets ragged in their throats.

Once there was quite a large crowd waiting to touch the magnificent back, so I quoted from *The Merchant of Venice:* "If you prick us, do we not bleed? If you poison us, do we not die? And if you wrong us, shall we not revenge?" The boss almost swallowed his tongue when he heard about it. I thought it added some sophistication and culture, but the boss claimed we make more money when I play the dumb brute, and he threatened to garner half my wages if I ever "pulled that stunt again."

Still, it's not that bad. The hay's changed every day, the meals are mostly hot, and Rita the Bearded Lady often brings a bottle over after work. We sit the whole night in front of the cage, talking and gazing up at the stars. Last week, in the dark, trembling, she put her hand on mine. She's in love with me. I could have her whenever I want. It won't take more than a few caresses to convince her to shave that pretty little beard of hers. She won't need it after she's been with me. I'll show her delights she's never dreamed of. To show her gratitude and her love, she'll please me in the most amazing ways I can imagine.

⌘

And suddenly, yesterday, everything here became illuminated with a beatific light. A dazzling, startling light. Tirza. Sweet, lovely little Tirza, the acrobat.

Oh, what little Tirza can do with her teeth, high above the center ring, without a net. Oh, how those muscled thighs and buttocks tighten under those darling outfits her aunt designs especially for her. How her tiny breasts, so perfectly round, show off her flat, muscled abdomen. Little Tirza makes my heart beat and my back stiffen. How I long for the lovely Tirza.

She hasn't noticed me yet. Her uncle Rubicon keeps an obsessive watch over her. He escorts her everywhere. I've heard that she sleeps in the same bed with her aunt. She's never alone, sweet Tirza. With these gypsies, that can only mean one thing: no one's had her.

Be still, my hammering heart.

One day, after I've had my fill of Rita the Bearded Lady, I'll make sure that darling Tirza in her glittering sequins and shiny tights catches a glimpse of my back, and... oh, how my back swells and aches at the thought, how it longs for the touch of those delicate fingers, those full blushing lips, that teasing pink tongue. Oh, Tirza, my blood sings for you, my back stretches and yearns.

⌘

We can be patient, my humped back and I. We'll not make the same mistake with Tirza that we made with Elena. It's enough to know that under those sparkling sequins, within those glamorous tights, our adorable Tirza is like all the rest, and no innocent Juliet ever spied a fairer, more devoted Romeo. *Vincenzo Magnifico. Vincenzo Glorioso. Vincenzo Passionato.*

Tirza, I worship you. I adore you. How happy my back and I will be when we have you all to ourselves. How glorious it will be when you're finally here with us, under the moonlight, inside the bars where I can show you love as you've never imagined.

And you will be with us.

We know it.

Povero cor di donna, eh?

If Vincenzo and his magnificent back know anything, it's how to make a woman happy. The woman hasn't been born who's indifferent to our charms. The woman hasn't been born whom we couldn't please. We love them all, my great back and I. We make every one of them deliriously happy. We make each of them ours, forever. They never want to leave us, they adore us so much. And we worship them in return. The memory of each one who came before not only makes my heart beat faster, my back stiffen and rise, but it makes each new woman all the more exciting.

Ah, yes, my dearest, darling, Tirza, life is sweet.

And when I have you all to myself, *cara mia,* life will be sweeter still.

VC in the USA

*T*hings were never the same after the Morrison twins got killed. Even David O'Donovan's dad couldn't go around actively supporting the war if he didn't want to hurt Doc Morrison. Of course, Mr. O'Donovan never came right out and said he opposed our country's involvement in Vietnam, but after the twins died, he stopped going around in his World War II uniform, and he hung the flag outside his house halfway down its wooden pole like everybody else in town did. We all respected him for that. We knew how hard it was for Mr. O'Donovan to change his mind about anything. I spent my entire childhood with the war in Vietnam, and it wasn't till I was 18 that the war ended. Then, when I was 38, the war in Vietnam came back to the United States.

I don't know exactly when the Vietnam war started: it'd been around as long as I could remember. Vietnam was there when me and my best friend Eddie Madison spooked that horse on the ridge, and it ran out on the freeway and got run over. Vietnam was there when I broke my collarbone falling out of the top bunk at Eddie's house, when Eddie's mom got terminal breast cancer, and when my dad went out for cigarettes and never came back.

Vietnam was there when men burned their draft cards and women took off their bras in public and dropped them in fiery metal trashcans. Vietnam was there when President Kennedy got killed, and when his brother Bobby, too, was shot. It was there when Malcolm X was murdered, and when Martin Luther King got assassinated.

Vietnam was on college campuses and in bars and in grocery stores all over the country. It was on Walter Cronkite every night and in all the magazines and newspapers. But the Vietnam war didn't really come to our town till the Morrison twins got drafted.

❀

I'd always thought that brothers or only sons couldn't go to Vietnam 'cause if they got killed, the family wouldn't have any sons left, but both the Morrisons went, and nobody thought for one single minute that they shouldn't. Mr. O'Donovan shook their hands right in the middle of Main Street, like he'd forgotten all about the time they egged his house and car on Halloween, like he'd forgotten how they used to bully his crippled son David.

Doc Morrison went around with a pin of the American flag in the lapel of his white coat, and everybody in the bar stood him and the twins drinks whenever they came in. Everybody knew that Spanky and Mouth Morrison were doing the right thing, the patriotic thing. Everybody except my mom.

"If they was my boys, I'd send them to Canada," she said, shaking her head and sighing every time she saw one of the twins in the grocery. "Terrible shame to risk them two fine boys. Doc really oughta send them to Canada, the both of them."

I begged Mom not to talk about Canada to the people in her check-out line. I didn't want them to think I was some yellow-bellied, snake-livered coward, but Mom kept on telling every single customer in her lane that if the war in Vietnam wasn't won by the time I turned 18, she was sending me to Canada if she had to knock me out, tie me up, put me in the trunk, and drive me over the border herself. Since everybody knew I was an only child and that my dad had disappeared years before, they knew why Mom said that. Still, it made me ashamed.

Every one of us had a duty to fight in Vietnam. At least, that's what we thought. That is, that's what we thought until the Morrison twins came back from their first tour of duty.

❀

There aren't words enough to say how they'd changed.

It wasn't the fact that they didn't drag-race out on abandoned Route 42 anymore, or the fact that they didn't play practical jokes any longer. It wasn't the fact that their heads were virtually shaved, or that they had identical tattoos on their arms. It wasn't the fact that they were harder and leaner now, or that they didn't have to smoke their cigarettes behind Old Lady Wilson's barn. It wasn't even the fact that now nobody could tell Spanky and Mouth apart anymore, not even Doc Morrison himself.

It was their eyes that showed how those twins had changed. Their eyes, and the way those eyes looked at you. Sometimes it made your knees all rubbery, and sometimes it made you shiver like you just walked over your own grave. Even Eddie Madison got spooked when he looked at the twins' eyes, and Eddie wasn't afraid of anything. Those eyes made Old Lady Wilson so nervous she crossed herself and hurried over to the other side of the street every time she saw one of the twins. Those eyes made somebody anonymously send each of the twins a Bible, which got left at home when the twins went back for their second tour of duty.

When Spanky or Mouth Morrison looked at you after they first came back from Vietnam, you knew something bad had happened over there. But if the two of them ever looked at you both at the same time, that was when you knew that no matter what had happened in that war, you didn't want to know about it. That was the thing that made you glad the twins weren't doing anything with their guns except cleaning them. That was the thing that made people start listening to Mom, asking her how she got her bank account at Canadian Savings and Trust, and what was the fastest route to get across the border to Canada.

The Morrison twins didn't ever talk to anyone about Vietnam, and they didn't come back from their second tour of duty. Doc Morrison threw away the American flag pin and grieved so much he became "Old" Doc Morrison overnight.

Mom started working extra hours at the grocery, to save more money to send to her Canadian bank account, and after Eddie Madison's only brother got killed in Vietnam, I started to put some of my money from my paper route in that account, without Mom's having to ask me.

Eddie went around punching walls and kicking fences and saying how he'd show those Viet Cong a thing or two just as soon as he was old enough, but the war ended right after Eddie and me turned 18, so we didn't lose any more of us than we already had.

I thought when the war ended that it was over, at least for those of us who hadn't gone. It was only after I had children of my own that the Vietnam war came over to the United States.

❀

One holiday weekend when we were supposed to go visit my ailing mother, the kids were sick, so Pam stayed home with our twins, and I visited Mom by myself.

One night after Mom had gone to bed and I'd run out of cigarettes, I went to the all-night convenience store near the new freeway. There were a few other people in the store: a short woman was in line in front of me, holding a box of cereal and carton of milk; the girlfriend of the teenage clerk stood over by the magazine rack, flipping through the magazines and blowing kisses at the clerk; a tall man in army fatigues opened and closed all the doors to the freezer section, without getting anything out.

The clerk was just ringing up the short woman's milk and cereal when the man in the army fatigues lurched over to us. When he got closer, I saw that he only had half an arm, and his limp was so pronounced, I wondered how he could walk at all. He leaned over the short woman in front of me and growled at her.

"God-damned Gook," he said, and everyone looked up at him.

The clerk stood there, with his cash register drawer and his mouth hanging open. His girlfriend looked up from her magazine. Without saying anything, the short woman tried to move away. The tall man stepped closer to her, leaning over her in a scary way.

"Damned Gook," he said. "We shoulda taken you out with the rest of them."

"I no Vietnamee," said the woman, looking over at the clerk. "I American citizen."

"The hell you are," said the man. "I'd know that damned Gook face and accent anywhere."

"My hup-band US citizen," she said, lowering her body away from his. "I US citizen, too."

"The hell you say. We shoulda Napalmed the shit outta every stinking one of you."

The woman turned around to me. When she tried to step closer, the vet blocked her. She spoke to me.

"No Vietnamee. No Gook. I born Korea."

"You can't fool me, you filthy, stinking Gook," he said. "Look what you did to me."

"Hey, come on, man," I said.

When he looked at me, I saw the twins' eyes instead of his. I stepped back, sweat suddenly drenching me. The clerk's girlfriend picked up an umbrella, holding it like a sword in front of her. The pimply-faced clerk reached beneath the counter, grabbed a pistol, cocked it, and pointed it at the vet. The short woman shrieked as she held onto me with both hands. The vet laughed when he saw the clerk, who stood there trembling, his teeth clenched so hard, I could see the muscles vibrating under the skin of his face.

"What the hell you think you're gonna do with that, you little punk?"

"You get outta here," said the clerk, "or I will shoot you down."

The vet started laughing as he grabbed the short woman by her hair and yanked her closer to the counter.

"You think you could hit a Gook with that thing, punk?"

"I think I could hit you, you sonofabitch. You're a lot bigger target, and I'm guessing you ain't got no bulletproof vest on neither."

The clerk, who had been shaking slightly, grew calmer the longer he kept the gun pointed at the vet's chest. The vet stopped laughing. He stopped smiling. He stepped closer to the counter, without letting go of the woman's hair. She was crying and screaming.

"I could break her neck before you shot me," he said.

"I'll still shoot you dead, man."

"No Gook. No Vietnamee," said the woman, sobbing.

"Come on, man. You heard her: she said she's not Vietnamese. Let her go, and get out of here," said the girlfriend, stepping closer with her umbrella, aiming its metal tip below his belt, between his legs. "You got anything left there, I'll hit it so hard, you'll go down."

"I don't wanna shoot you, buddy, but I gotta tell you: I been dying to shoot a robber."

The girlfriend nodded as the clerk licked his lips. Suddenly, both of them were looking out of the Morrison twins' eyes, too.

"What the hell's the matter with you? Are you all rice-eating VCs in training or something? She's a Gook. I'm an American. This is what she did to me."

"I *so* want to shoot you, man," said the clerk. "I'd be a hero. Saving the store's cash *and* saving a poor old woman that you attacked."

The vet pushed the woman away from him so hard that she fell into me. His narrowed eyes strafed us. For the first time in more than twenty years, I found myself trying to pray. The vet lurched away. The gun's muzzle and the umbrella's metal tip kept their aim on him constantly.

"Goddamned buncha Gook-lovers," he said before he slammed out of the store.

After the man had gotten into his pickup and left, the clerk uncocked his gun and put it back under the counter.

"Would you really have shot him?" I said.

"I ain't gonna let no asshole hurt no woman," he said.

"Neither am I," said his girlfriend as she put down the umbrella near the front door.

"I no Vietnamee," said the woman, still clinging to my arm. "I no Gook. My hup-band US GI. We marry long time. I in US twenty-five year."

The clerk bagged the milk and cereal, the cash register beeped and whirred when I paid for my cigarettes. The clerk's hands were shaking slightly when he gave me my change. The girlfriend, with a grim look on her face, nodded to me as I went to the door.

The old woman, her bag crushed to her chest, stood there, peering anxiously out at the parking lot. When she looked up at me, I saw the same thing in her eyes that I'd seen in the vet's eyes, the same thing I'd seen in the clerk's and his girlfriend's eyes, the same thing I'd seen so many years before in the Morrison twins' eyes.

"No Vietnamee," the old woman said. "Hate Vietnamee. Hate VC. Hate Gook."

"It's okay, little Grandmother," said the clerk's girlfriend. "This nice man will walk you to your car. You will, won't you, Mister? In case that asshole is still out there waiting."

I nodded.

"See? He's a nice man. He'll make sure you get to your car safe."

I walked her to her car, stood beside it till she'd locked the doors, started the engine, and driven away. I stayed in the parking to make sure the pickup didn't follow her. Then I walked home to my Mom's house.

❀

I couldn't sleep that night. I sweated so much the sheets got damp, and the cool night air blowing over my skin made me shiver. I smoked so many cigarettes that Mom complained she could smell the smoke through the bedroom walls, so I went out to sit on the front porch.

It was dark and quiet out there, but my arms and legs felt like they were wound tight, ready to snap. When a car backfired, I jumped up out of the porch-swing and squatted down behind the rails of the front porch. After I called Pam again, she threatened to bundle up the twins and drive up to Mom's that very minute unless I convinced her I was really all right. I promised to get some sleep and call her back in the morning.

After I smoked the last cigarette, I went back to the convenience store. The glare of the lights hurt my eyes. Nobody was there but the teenaged clerk. I walked up and down the aisles for a while, looking for something, anything, I don't know what. Finally I went to the checkout and asked for cigarettes. The clerk shifted his eyes away from mine as he rang them up. Though I held out my hand, he put my change on the counter. The walk home to Mom's house was too short, and I was still on the front porch when the sun came up.

❀

I don't know why I never told anyone about this — not Mom or Pam or even Eddie. I tried to tell Eddie once, years afterward, and as I was dialing him up in Deadwood, it seemed to me that if anybody understood, it'd be Eddie. I never did tell him, though. When I called, Jeannie'd just left him and taken the kids, and the war seemed lifetimes away. I promised to come see him the next summer, and he promised to write more often.

Sometimes I lie awake at night because I can't hear anything but that vet's voice, because I can't smell anything but fear, because I can't see anything except the Morrison Brothers' eyes.

I wonder constantly why I didn't protect that woman, why I didn't stand up to that vet, why I let those young kids who hadn't even been born during the Vietnam War stand up to him instead.

Was I afraid that if I'd protected that poor old Vietnamese woman, I'd somehow betray Spanky and Mouth Morrison, Eddie Madison's big brother, David O'Donovan's cousin, and all the others I'd known who'd died there?

Did I think if I protected an old Vietnamese woman, we'd forget all those who'd been maimed and wounded and broken in the fighting, that we wouldn't recall those captured or lost or missing in the dense and deadly jungles?

Did I think if I showed empathy or compassion to one old woman whose people had once been our enemy, that those of us who never came back would suddenly become forever lost?

Nothing more than shadows.

Nothing more than carved names on black marble.

No longer missed, no longer remembered, no longer loved.

About Alexandria

Alexandria Constantinova Szeman

Critically acclaimed & award-winning author, Alexandria Constantinova Szeman (formerly writing as "Sherri" Szeman because her 1st editor told her that her name "wouldn't fit on the book cover," & wanted an "easy" first name to go with her "hard" last name) began as a poet before she started writing novels, short fiction, and creative writing books.

Szeman has Ph.D.'s in Creative Writing and in English & Comparative World Literatures. Her dissertation, *Survivor: One Who Survives* (University of Cincinnati, 1986) was a collection of original poetry, all of which were accepted or published by university & literary journals before her dissertation defense. While in graduate school, her poetry was awarded numerous prizes, including The Elliston Poetry Prize (several times) & The Isabel and Mary Neff Creative Writing Fellowship.

Her first novel, *The Kommandant's Mistress*, on the Holocaust from multiple points of view and perspectives, was chosen as one of *The New York Times Book Review*'s "Top 100 Books of the Year" (1993). It was also awarded the University of Rochester's (NY) prestigious Kafka Prize "for the outstanding book of prose fiction by an American woman" (1994), and Central State University's (OH) Talmadge McKinney Research Award (1993).

Originally published by HarperCollins (1993) & HarperPerennial (1994), the novel has been sold to publishers in 10 foreign countries and translated into French, Spanish, Russian, Lithuanian, Danish, Swedish, Norwegian, among others. It was republished by Arcade (2000) & was optioned for film (though funded, it was never made).

Her second novel, *Only with the Heart,* on the devastating effects of Alzheimer's on a family, is on the recommended reading lists of Alzheimer's Associations nationwide. Originally published by Arcade (2000), the Revised & Expanded, 12th Anniversary Edition contains new scenes with updated medical treatment/medications for Alzheimer's, as well as new legal definitions and statutes regarding assisted suicide.

Her third novel, *No Feet in Heaven,* about two brothers and their female cousin who decide to attain fame by hunting down a notorious serial killer themselves, won praise from several NY editors before it was accepted by a New York Trade House; unfortunately, that House was purchased by a larger NY Trade House: the editor was then laid off, and the book "rejected."

The titular story in her award-winning collection of short stories, *Naked, with Glasses,* won Third Prize in *Story Magazine*'s "Seven Deadly Sins Contest" (1995), and the manuscript won the Grand

Prize in the UKA Press [United Kingdom Authors Press] 2007 Annual International Writing Competition.

Her two poetry collections, *Love in the Time of Dinosaurs* and *Where Lightning Strikes: Poems on the Holocaust,* both contain critically acclaimed & award-winning poems. Each volume includes several poems from her dissertation, *Survivor: One Who Survives* (University of Cincinnati, 1986). The poems have won several prizes, including University of Cincinnati's Elliston Prize (anonymous competition; 1983, 1984, 1985), an Honorable Mention in the Chester H. Jones Poetry Foundation National Poetry Competition (1985), Michigan State University's *The Centennial Review* Michael Miller Award for Poetry (1985), an Honorable Mention in *Writer's Digest* National Writing Competition (1980), and The Isabel & Mary Neff Fellowship for Creative Writing (1984-85). Both volumes were unanimously accepted for publication by all outside readers of UKA Press [United Kingdom Authors Press] in 2004.

Szeman is currently completing her latest novel, as well as revising her memoir (about growing up with a mother who practiced Munchausen's by Proxy), and is about to publish several creative writing exercise books, including an e-book version of her classic *Mastering Point of View* (originally published by Story Press, 2001).

Alexandria's Amazon Author Central Page
Amazon.com/author/alexandriaszeman

Alexandria's Web-Site
AlexandriaConstantinovaSzeman.com

Read excerpts from all her books:
AlexandriaConstantinovaSzeman.com/Books.php

Alexandria's Blog: The Alexandria Papers
TheAlexandriaPapers.com
AlexandriaConstantinovaSzeman.com/Blog.php

Alexandria's Twitter @Alexandria_SZ
Twitter.com/Alexandria_SZ
AlexandriaConstantinovaSzeman.com/Twitter.html

Contact Alexandria
AlexandriaConstantinovaSzeman.com/Contact.php

www.ingramcontent.com/pod-product-compliance
Lightning Source LLC
Chambersburg PA
CBHW030623130626
46552CB00002B/687